Scotch mc Bride

DEADLY

John Pirillo

Copyright 2020

"It's long been said that the white shark is the most deadly fish of the sea and man's worst nightmare.

But truly, Watson, the most deadly animal walks on two feet, not swims in the ocean or sea."

-- Sherlock Holmes

DARK DEEDS

She walked past him, not even seeing him. The early morning was shrouded by thick, angry clouds, and her view was limited. He was hidden deep in the shades of the morning mist and the huddled buildings that clung to each other for comfort, affording the monster hiding places within deep and dark shadows. Making it easy for him not to be seen or even noticed. And the walk was past buildings so beaten and worn by time and salt that there was no reason to look for more than rot and ruin: salt and wind. Wind and salt had stricken this area permanently, it seemed.

What he thought she wouldn't have been able to know one iota better even had she spotted him and the odd device he clutched between the fingers of both hands.

Not a remarkable looking man even out of the shadows, he huddled there, waiting to ply his secret trade. Life. Not the giving of it.

He checked the blades he had loaded into the ammo clip of his weapon and smiled. The first time was more demanding, he thought. He found that sexual reference somewhat amusing, even if darkly malicious and foreboding.

She got far enough away from him that he felt comfortable trailing her. He found it amusing, stalking her like a hunter in the wee hours of the morning in a forest. Except, here, the forest was abandoned shops. Massive warehouses that had seen better days. And here, sleeping homeless saw him coming, but pretended they didn't and huddled further into the very shadows he trod. Trembling, shaking in fear.

They were nothing to him. So, he ignored the vermin. No, today, he had bigger fish to fry. And he was following her. Allowing her the few last moments of serenity, the poor creature might harbor before she was dispatched into the darkness he envied. The deep shadowy recesses of life he honored now with his hunt.

Anyone trying to analyze him would be fraught with confusion, for, on the surface, he didn't appear to be a killer, a ruthless murderer.

He wasn't.

Yet!

A DATE WITH DESTINY

Margery Thumwalt shrugged deeper into her coat. Trying to beat back the bitter, freezing cold storming off the Thames this morning. It felt like a ravaging monster threatening her and her fellow citizens with chapped lips and cheeks from its icy touch. Even death if one stopped to rest in it.

"Dratted wind!" She cursed; she didn't really mean it. She loved the wind. It made her feel alive and vital. Something her life lacked considerably at this time. She was heading for her work at the fishery, where fresh seafood was prepared for the marketplace. She cut off their tails and heads and made sure they were placed correctly in the labeled buckets of ice for them to later be used for the cat food that would be processed from their remains.

It was not a very interesting job. And if one didn't pay one's minds closely enough to the job, they could end up with a lost finger or worse, like poor old Clement had last spring and had to retire early because he could no longer do the job.

No pension.

Barely any pay.

It was a bottom end job with no future and no prospects of getting any better. Fish were becoming scarcer. They were retreating from the toxic waste offshore pouring into the Thames and Atlantic from the factories still using coal for fuel. And since no one was making sure they didn't overfish the schools that swam offshore, they were becoming even more scarce every year. Fishing had a dismal future. For her, an even darker end with few jobs and low pay on top of that.

She sighed with a touch of grief and longing that most do these days when faced with a dreary and seemingly hopeless future. And yet, she and others like her clung to thin threads of hope that it would somehow miraculously change for the better.

From reports coming over from the Yanks, it didn't look much better for them as well. The big ones that ran that country, and it seems most of the planet, had little desire to share their wealth. She could understand that. Where she worked was no different. The upper bosses milked their workers of every dreg of strength, paid them little, watched them wither and fall away, and said nothing.

To weed out these darker thoughts, her mind drifted towards her love life. Single, with not much hope of marriage now in her later years, she smiled at several children who passed at a run for school. It reminded her of what was best in life. Life should be filled with growth, exploration, knowledge, fulfillment, and happiness. It should not be an endless tide of longing and grief that swept higher and higher day by day, as one watched the rich become more prosperous and one's own life more flawed, more challenging. Not aware of it yet, these children lived on the edge of hope for a better future, not even aware that it might instead be a dark one.

Probably going to be tardy. But maybe the children would make it in time and over time, even as she believed she would.

She smiled again, remembering her own such years and how she had such big dreams for her future. She had seen herself married...to a man who would love and protect her. She would live in a fine house. It would have the finest furniture and be filled with warmth and charm. She would have three demanding children who hopped, skipped, and pulled on her apron to hurry up and make their dinner. She saw herself doing the daily laundry. Pushing and pulling at soaked sweaters and socks, hammering their moisture away, before pinning them to a homemade clothesline secure enough to bear their burden until dry.

But that hadn't happened.

***

Her man, Jeffrey Thumwalt, had shipped to sea to serve in the war in Afghanistan.

She still remembered their last conversation, even though it pinched her heart to do so.

"It's not a picnic, or a party, Jeffie. It's war. Scoundrels killing scoundrels. Confused souls battering each other for power over each other."

He laughed.

"Sounds like all wars, my pretty. Men don't really die in wars to defend the honor of their country so much these days, as they do to protect the wealth of the wealthier."

He looked sour for a moment, and then spit into the dirt. "Sad, but true. We, the people of the earth, are becoming servants again. Just like in the days of the aristocracy, when Kings and Queens ruled."

"Then why are you doing it?" She had demanded.

"Because if I don't, we'll never have enough." He took her hands between his and pressed them close to his heart. "My heart aches at leaving you, but it aches even more at the idea of our children having nothing because I have no skills to lift them...and you up."

She had thrown herself against him. "I don't care if we're poor; I'll have you."

He gently tilted her face and kissed her lightly on the lips. "And that's what I love about you, my lassie. You care more about what's real than what's not."

"Jeffie!"

He held a finger to her lip to stop her next words.

"Don't you worry your pretty little head, my dear Margie. I will never get a foot near where the action is anyway. That I can promise."

Then he had hiked his luggage with his hands, given her one last long, long kiss, then winked at her and trod to the waiting transport to fly away forever.

He didn't see any action. It saw him.

He was blown up by a roadside bomb. Two of them on either side, interconnected so that their explosives would crush whatever were between them.

It had been his supply truck.

He and ten other men had been torn to pieces by the shrapnel from the bombs and bled to death if they still had any life remaining in them before help could reach them.

She sighed and wrapped her arms about herself, trying to hug the pain of those memories from her.

Vengeance?

Who knew for sure? He was just one of many who may have been at the right place at the wrong time.

He was dead now.

She?

Alone.

She swallowed the bitterness rising in her throat and shrugged her coat tighter.

She usually took a shortcut along the main route. She traveled by foot through a short alley—no reason to worry. The constables kept the area clear of any troublemakers or hooligans. And usually, the homeless who slept there kept any muggers away.

As she got halfway through the dark alley, she suddenly became aware that all the homeless were gone, or was it just her imagination.

No matter, she thought.

She shrugged off her sudden apprehension and continued towards her destination, the fishery, whose tall well-worn structure was clear to her eyes now in the near distance.

Then a swishing sound caught her attention.

She reached a hand up to her throat.

Her eyes rolled up in her head.

Her head and body separated.

Margery no longer had to worry about the future anymore.

TOO CLOSE FOR COMFORT

Scotch hitched his head aside, as usual, to watch as Inspector Dublin marched to work, passing the barbershop he was getting a close shave in. The man was fastidious to a second. Never missed his appointed time at work.

Scotch smiled and then noted the time on the clock ahead of him. He frowned. Ten minutes late.

No matter.

He yawned.

"Be still, Scotch!" His barber warned, or I'll slice half your ear off."

Scotch laughed. "Then, I'll have half an ear more to listen with."

"You're impossible," his barber shot back, amusement in his voice.

Scotch didn't nod as he was wont to do when sporting in bouts of humor. He, indeed, might have lost part of his ear at that moment as the barber's blade played hopscotch about the base of his ear.

Scotch was starving. He hadn't eaten for hours. He had to get the haircut, and the only way to get it was to leave early from home. His barber was booked heavily later on. Besides which, he was starting to look as mangy as a mongrel dog. But he had swung by the market next door and grabbed a sandwich they had prepared for customers like him on the run and stuffed it into his right trench coat pocket.

Later, me lass! He thought to his hidden sandwich.

It was a chicken sandwich—the last one. So at least that part of his day was off to a good start. But these thoughts put his mouth to watering again. He had to lick away the saliva starting to drool from his mouth as the barber finished his neck.

Finished, the barber held up a hand mirror. Scotch took it and examined the front of his face and then the sides, using the fixed mirror opposite his chair to see it.

"What do you think, Scotch?"

Scotch turned his head left and right. "Perfect, but a bit too tidy now," he said with his usual Scottish burr that softened every word he spoke like a muffler was put on them.

The barber looked on in horror at his client, Scotch McBride. The young man was a blondish-haired rogue of a detective. He always seemed to wear a perpetual five-day-old beard, a sheepish grin, and a face with amused eyes that rarely looked directly at you. And his hair was mussed up as if fresh from a rainstorm or shower. Not perfect looking, but it didn't seem to bother the man one bit.

Scotch looked again in the mirror, smiling. "Perfect. Don't want to look too good, the perps will think I'm a detective or worse yet, one of those Hollywood types straight off the plane to tour London."

His barber sighed. "That took me all of thirty minutes to get it perfect."

"Perfection is in the eye of the beholder," Scotch reminded his barber with a wry grin. Then he got off his barber chair, thumped his shoes three times on the paneled floor to get any loose hair off him, and then turned to his barber. "No harm, no foul, Mister Ray," Scotch said in his Scottish burr, "But Me hair loves its freedom as much as your scissors and razor love cutting it away. Not to mention your sometimes overly eager bottle of mousse and hairspray.

The barber shrugged. He knew it was no use arguing with Scotch by now. Three years the customer and three years the same routine had built a foundation of mutual friendship that neither wanted to change. It had become a comfortable battleground between the two of them, replacing the usual barbershop banter he had with many of his other customers.

Scotch eyed himself in the barber's mirror, and then suddenly, he stiffened. Someone had just run past the display window. The faint barking of a dog could be heard as he vanished.

He threw a note down on the counter and ran out the door. "Next week!" He yelled over his shoulder.

"Gotcha down!" His barber assured him, and then Scotch was out the door and hit the sidewalk pavement at a run.

The man he had been trailing for days, months now had just run past, chased by a mongrel dog of all things.

"Hey!" He hollered after the man.

The man looked over his shoulder.

The mongrel caught up and bit his right ankle.

Scotch grabbed the man by both his arms and wrestled him to the ground until he could get the cuffs on him.

"What do you think you're doing?"

The mongrel kept tearing at the man's right ankle, determined to make a meal of it evidently.

"Putting you right as rain," Scotch hissed.

Finished, he rose to his feet, and then jerked the man to his. He eyed him with that slanted angle of his head he was in the habit of doing, his eyes not on the man's face, but on his neck. "For robbery and the beating of animals."

"I plead guilty to the last, especially this one!" The man growled, trying to kick the mongrel from his right ankle.

Scotch looked down. "Easy, boy. I've got the lad now."

The mongrel let go. Sat upon its haunches, giving Scotch a happy wigwag of his tail up and down over and over, his tongue lolling out from his mouth happily. He barked once and then rolled over.

Scotch eyed the dog. "Think you've caught me now, just like I caught this blighter, do you?"

The dog sat up, its tail thumping the pavement energetically, then raised up on its haunches and made a begging motion with its paws.

Scotch groaned.

The dog's nose was sniffing the air. It barked eagerly, an expectant and hopeful look on its face.

Scotch sighed and then reached into his coat pocket for the sandwich.

Before he could offer it to the dog, it leaped into the air and snatched it from his hand. It landed at his feet, nuzzled up against him, and hungrily began wolfing the sandwich down, paper and all.

The thief roared with laughter. Then said, "I may go to jail, but you're going to be in jail forever with that Muff!"

And to prove him right or wrong, depending on one's point of view, the dog left its meal and bit the thief on his left ankle.

"Hey!" Scotch hollered out.

The mongrel gave him a doggie smile and then went back to eating again.

The thief eyed the dog sourly, then Scotch, but said nothing more.

Scotch smiled.

"Muff. I think I like that name. Fits ye."

The dog barked, wagged its tail in acknowledgment, rolled over on its back, then back to its feet and grabbed up the remainder of its meal, and wagged its tail.

"See!" The thief remarked. "You've named him. Once you name them, you can never get rid of them. It's like getting married."

Scotch smiled at that, then grabbed the thief by his collar and urged him forward. "Tell that to the Inspector; he's married."

Scotch grinned real big into the man's face. "I'm as sure as rain that he will be loving ye for saying that."

INSPECTOR DUBLIN

The thief was grabbed by his right and left arms and led from the front desk past Inspector Dublin, who eyed Scotch thoughtfully.

"New hair cut?"

"Every month."

"Mmmm."

Scotch eyed the Inspector as he rubbed at the back of his neck, his other hand resting on his stomach, which almost looked as if he were trying to keep it from getting away from him.

The man had quite an appetite from what Scotch had heard and seen.

"We've been trying to nail that one for months now. Slicker blighter I've never seen."

"Aye, that he was," Scotch reminded the Inspector.

Inspector Dublin rubbed at his bloodshot eyes.

"Ye really should sleep more, Inspector."

"I would, but London is one helluva mess these days, and I can't take my eyes off it for one hour, and something else pops up I need to attend to. Hell, Scotch, you look like a train wreck yourself."

Scotch grinned. "Hopefully, a well-rewarded one."

Inspector Dublin too the cue. He shook a finger at the clerk nearest him. "Get this man the reward!"

The clerk ran off to the banking clerk to get a check for Scotch.

"You know, we could use a man like you on the force, Mister McBride."

"I'm sure ye could, but I'm afraid my sleeping hours would interfere with yer good graces."

Inspector Dublin's stern face creased with a smile. He adjusted his black tie over his starched white shirt and shrugged. "Your loss."

Bark.

Bark.

Bark.

Inspector Dublin looked past Scotch and saw the mongrel dog he had fed.

"Your new girlfriend?"

The dog bared its teeth.

Scotch grinned. "Mustn't speak unkindly of our four-footed friends, Inspector, or it might come back and bite ye."

The Inspector cocked an eyebrow, indicating he wasn't amused, then nodded and walked off. Work to be done.

Scotch turned to leave just as the clerk came running back with a check.

"You're an angel! God bless ye, sir!"

The clerk smiled and then walked away.

Scotch kissed the check and then leaned over to stroke the mongrel dog on its head. "Dog food."

The dog barked.

"Come on, Muff, we got to do some shopping. "

The newly named Muff proudly strutted alongside Scotch as he made his way for the entrance to the Yard, constables, and clerks all smiling at the dog as it passed.

NO WAY OUT

Four hookers, fondly called Midnight Rangers in the town of London these days, smoked cigarettes, chatted softly, and shrugged light shawls about their shoulders. It wasn't much, but it helped stave off the worst of the night chill from their cold, miserable bodies.

Life was not easy for them.

You might see a movie about a happy hooker who marries a good-hearted rich man. Still, the truth is they are disrespected, even though seen as a desired necessity by those who use and abuse them.

A world that fights to fill the coffins of the few while denying themselves and hoping their turn will come next has no love for these women of the night. They are looked down upon and trampled by society.

So, lacking any safe place to go. Abandoned, seemingly by those they loved...parents, brothers, sisters... life! They had little hope of peace and comfort. And would most likely die alone and unloved, by family and fate, except by those who shared the same small beach of exile from the so-called real world.

Not one of them worried at that moment that it might not be their last, nor that it might be the curtain closing of life never wrought that well to begin with. No, they just savored the brief moments of comradery they shared before some stranger, or an old client, drove up, walked up, or hobbled up to take them one by one to another place. For a time. For pleasure. For money.

Perhaps even a lot of money.

But just as possibly, much pain and abuse.

It was a gambler's life they led, and sometimes you won, and sometimes you lost. Big time!

This was such a time.

Swish!

The tallest of the women turned about at the sound of a frightening sucking sound on her right. The woman next to her had her head cut off at the shoulders. Her head had been severed from its root and lay at her feet. A moment later, her body tumbled to the floor next to her head. A blur flashed in the air and struck the next woman, then the next, sending their heads plunging to the floor. Whatever had made the cuts had moved so fast the eye couldn't follow it or make it out clearly.

Her other two friends made to let out a scream before the cuts, but the same blade sliced through their throats, severing their heads and the tall one, frozen to that moment, stepped back, but not to freedom.

Something sharp pierced her throat as well, and her struggles to make a living, to find some kind of happiness and fulfillment in her meager world...they vanished forever!

"Muff!" I hissed.

The mongrel I had befriended earlier that day hopped onto the bench beside me and began eating from the bowl I had made for the tyke.

It was filled with scraps of chicken, mashed up potatoes and peas, and a dash of sugar to sweeten the sour parts.

Muff wagged its tail and smashed its snout into the food, then backed away a moment, as if to say, "Hey, what are ye pulling on me?"

I dipped my right forefinger into the mashed potatoes and then licked it.

"Yum!"

Muff resumed his position at the bowl and ate away until even the bowl's grease spots were licked clean and gone.

Muff sat up again and eyed me with those big, beautiful brown eyes of his. He twitched his rump and then wagged his tail. "Come on, Scotch!" He urged in that way all doggies, bless their wee hearts, does.

I grinned and emptied my water glass into the bowl.

Muff barked several times in approval and began making the most of the water as well as he had his meal. The only thing he didn't like was the lemon slice.

I always put a slice of lemon in my water. Anything I drink pretty much. It's good for ye.

I grinned happily.

"Looks like I've found Meself another friend, lad."

Muff looked up and barked.

I grinned.

"Remind me of a friend of mine, Muff."

Muff looked up from his drinking, wagged his tail, and then barked, "Yes!" in that way, all dogs do when ye talk to them that way.

"I'll drink to that and raise ye one," I said.

Otter, Scotch's friend and partner, a big man with a big heart, but a mouth always tuck on open, eyed me with a cigar clenched between his teeth.

His right hand clenched a beer mug, which was frothing over. He sipped it quick, sat down opposite me. "Who's your new girlfriend, Scotch?"

I laughed.

Muff, pretty sure we were talking about him, sat up proud and said nothing. He had doggie's right to brag, and in this case, it meant showing his happy teeth, but not growling.

Otter eyed the game board we had been playing on before he went for a fresh beer. He scowled at the blue-chip I had lain down—the winning position as usual.

"You sucker-punched me again, Scotch."

He stuck his cigar in the mug of beer, slapped down a twenty, and stormed off, looking for fresh beer, a hot babe, and someone else to entertain for the night. He didn't have enough patience to win, and he knew it, but he was always game enough to try. I give him credit for that.

Most people look at him and wonder why I put up with such a scoundrel. Me, I look at him and think how lucky I am to have such a friend.

He would throw himself in front of a bullet for me. I know this because he has. He has a nice, neat puncture scar over his right nipple where he had caught one.

Fortunately, it wasn't a hollow point or a powerful enough caliber to penetrate his breast bone. Still, it was strong enough to leave its autograph.

So I tolerated him—a lot.

Just like Otter tolerated me as well.

You see, I'm an enigma to most, even to myself. I'm a P.I., a private eye. It's what I do for a living, such as it is. When I'm not working a case, which is not as often as I'd like, I get bored.

Then I haunt bookstores for old manuscripts that might be of use. Look for basements in abandoned homes for sale. Chase down old attics cluttered with unopened boxes, trunks, and chests...looking for that heart of gold. Book, actually. The gold would come if I found the right ones.

You see, I'm a bit of a problem solver. No Sherlock Holmes for sure, but if that guy ever showed up, I suspect I might give him a good run for the money.

And books, especially old ones, can come in handy when you're dealing with particular problems. And I'm not talking about the kind of criminals you can cuff and put behind bars.

No, I'm talking about those that haunt the night and go bumping around there, seeking innocents.

"Hey, Blondie!"

I looked up from my musings.

She was a doll.

A real doll.

Four foot ten and all of her hot, hot, hot. And as Oriental, as they come. With oval almond eyes, olive skin, slender fingers, and a chest, I'd love to explore. Still, I'm not going anywhere I'm not wanted, so I keep that to myself. So don't you go talking to her behind my back, or I'll have to come looking for you.

Get it?

Got it.

Good.

So, here I was at Fantastic Freddie's again on late night Friday. Clueless and dateless.

I fiddled with my tea and coffee a moment. I love to mix two flavors of tea —Raspberry and chamomile. It helps me sleep and also adds something sweet to my taste. Almond coconut coffee for flavor and zest, with extra strong caffeine, added to keep me sharp and witty.

I pulled at my hair a bit—a nervous habit.

I also cocked my head.

Whenever I check myself out in a mirror. Which is not often, thank God! Never have been the kind to get lost in myself. I see Meself as a youngish man who could be in his thirties, maybe early forties, with a perpetual grin and look of amusement on his face.

Mind you now, it's not because I'm really amused at everything.

"Scotch," my mother would tell me as she scooted me out the front door for school. "Keep a smile in your heart and a grin on your lips, and you'll outlive your father."

I did.

And I rarely got in fights. Not my nature. I'm a solver, not a punisher. I don't need to be right, just because I usually am. I inherited that nature from my father, and it was enhanced by an older woman I know, whom I'll get into later on in this story.

Anyway, I had just gotten a case I had no idea how to solve. But I took it because I was desperate, and Otter threatened to win our games if I didn't get with it.

He had his eyes on me from the other side of the bar, where he was huddled between two Midnight Rangers. That's what we call hookers in these parts of London. Because they range the night, and usually it was Midnight or later, they appeared on the docks, at the pubs. Along with the street corners, dresses hiked up, revealing whatever amount of flesh it took to nab a new client or entice an old one back for another round of touching me for a price.

Yes, they were angels, all right. With hot dresses, flashing eyes, and hot pink lips, these angels will clasp onto yours for however long you wish to pay for.

In the newer Holmes books, they're called Midnight Angels. I wouldn't go that far. Some of them can kick your ass from here to Borneo. They're tough. Not all of them are, but most are. They have to be. These are modern times. The new criminals don't even have the most basic manners that Victorian London's old scumbags did.

I even know one Midnight Ranger who can drink Otter under the table, and arm wrestles him to the floor without blinking an eye.

I respect her a lot.

She ignores me.

She likes the rough and tumble kind and ones like Otter, who appear unpolished and rough on the outside, but got a heart of gold, or at least some sort of comparable metal.

I donated to them from time to time when I got lucky because I felt for them. It must hurt to make your living on your back most of the time and the knees as well, I'm told. I don't ask. I have learned to listen with not just my ears but with my heart.

Mostly.

Sometimes I don't smile.

I don't mix.

I don't laugh.

I just don't.

Don't.

Don't want anything more to do with my fellow men. They can be so downright sodden and disgusting at times.

Maybe that's how I got into this habit of kind of always averting my eyes, never looking someone straight in the face, playing with my hair. I know it's not what got me to eating Cinnamon Bears when I got nervous or was lonely.

I popped a Cinnamon Bear into my mouth, cocked my head, and averted my eyes as the sound of a woman tap-tapped in her high heels towards my booth. You'll usually see my head cocked. I have a medical condition: arthritis. I did it to myself when I was young. Took a terrible fall. But then you probably know that already if you're one of my friends.

I didn't even bother to look to see who it was. I could tell by her fragrance: sandalwood and roses.

Every Midnight Ranger has a distinct scent. And me the dog who can identify them all by their fragrance. An excellent tool to have when you're trying to sort out people quickly.

And in my line of work. Mostly murder crimes. In my line, you needed all the tools possible.

"Hey, Pearl!" I greeted.

She shuffled in her ten-inch spike shoes onto the bench across from me, bumping knees with me under the table. Purposefully.

I ignored it.

Pearl's not a flirt, but she knows how to get my heart pumping and adrenalin sizzling hot. Least, I think so. She never seemed interested when I suggested we spend some time together on a date. She never gave the ice cube treatment when I asked, but she didn't exactly break out the Bunsen burners to make my life any easier either. She was a lovely enigma that tugged at my heart.

I didn't look down any further than her neckline. Not because I'm a perv, but because I'm...I guess you could say shy, but I'd say...protective.

People can control you if they can connect to your eyes. I don't like being controlled, manipulated, and molded into someone's pet project or toy.

"So, what's up?" I finally said, after identifying her scent clearly, then noting the typical tattoo on her throat: a rose and a stick of incense burning behind it.

"You really like my rose, don't you?"

I almost looked up—the last thing I expected her to say. I shook my head. "Have to look some direction and don't want to look away, that would be rude."

She started to ask the question, most did, "How come you don't look in my face?"

She didn't.

I respected her more for not doing that than if she had. She knew that. She could read men, just like I could read criminal motivations and tendencies.

Give me a fingerprint, and I'll find a trail.

Give me a crime, and I'll nab the blighter happily. But her...not a clue where to start.

Simple as that.

She leaned closer, so I could smell the rose and sandalwood better. My hormones were screaming Bloody Mary, I want you so bad I can taste it, but I just kept my head averted.

"Don't go outside," she whispered.

My eyebrows rose like a pair of blonde crows elevating for the skies on those gorgeous obsidian black wings of theirs. "What?"

She almost got me to look her directly in the eyes with that remark. It was the last thing I expected her to say. I did get as far as her nose. Cute as a button. Smooth and sexy.

Can I help it if I love Oriental women? We all have our flaws, or maybe it was just Pearl. I've never had the time or opportunity to this point in my life to learn if it applied equally to all Oriental women...only Pearl.

She leaned so close over the table I could smell jasmine perfume she dotted behind each earlobe. And the dash she liberally, but pretty much carefully placed in that spot I dared not look. Ever. Not if I wanted to preserve my soul.

I love women.

Just don't want to be one.

Or to be with one.

Maybe Pearl.

Maybe.

Don't ask me why.

Not yet.

Maybe after some time, we've gotten to know each other. Well, perhaps then you can snake it out of me. Maybe not.

We'll see.

She grinned. She knew. Damn her all anyway. Such a tease, Damnit!

I'm not celibate. I got feelings, and I'm young enough to want to do something about it. I just don't want to take advantage of anyone or push for something that's not mine to have.

And like I said earlier, I don't want to be with women. Too much pain involved with relationships. Pearl had taught me that lesson.

And very well.

Does this mean I want to be with men?

I had to grin over that one.

Not a chance in hell. No problem with others doing that, but I'm strictly the opposite sex kind of guy.

"You shouldn't make fun of me, Scotch. I'm serious, you shouldn't go out tonight."

Once more, she startled me into almost looking into her eyes. I came closer. Just below her eyelids, but quickly averted my glance again, but this time to the bar where I noticed a large man with a hugely baggy coat by the door, surveying the place.

His eyes locked on my booth a moment. I'm sure he wasn't interested in me. His eyes only stopped on the women. And on Pearl.

I felt an instant dislike for the bugger, but I kept it drowned with a splash of healthy sanity. I'm not an impulsive man by nature, and I don't seek fights, except when it's in defense of someone.

She lost her grin and whispered, even lower. "They're out tonight." And this time, she punctuated her warning statement with such intensity, I actually looked up.

Briefly, but long enough to see, she was deadly serious. Although looking at me, it wasn't anything personal like I feared. It was...

Friendly.

I gave her a blank look. She'd never talked like this before. But then usually she's got other things on her mind on Friday nights and other people on her body as well.

Yeah. Pearl's a Midnight Ranger. But she's tough, resilient, and meticulous. No rubber. No ducky to play with.

I grinned.

"Don't laugh!" She scolded me.

I suddenly became aware I was staring into her face and filing away what I saw there. I instantly averted my face, anew.

The odd man was gone.

I told her the first thing that came to my mind. "It's not what you said, it's what you do."

She blushed, then pulled back and got up to leave.

"Hey, don't run off!" I begged her.

She gave me a hurt look. "I thought I was your friend, Scotch."

I didn't see it. I felt it.

That's something else about me; I'm empathic. I can feel what people are thinking, feeling. Sometimes it's a blessing in my line of work, but other times it's a curse. It's not always a good thing to know what another's thinking, feeling. I don't hear thoughts, but I sense thoughts as if they were my own.

Deeply.

I sighed. "Not my fault you're not mine."

She gave me another hurt look.

"I...I..." She began to wipe at tears in her eyes. "I can't do that with you, Scotch, I have too much history."

I tried to grab her arm, to reassure her it wasn't what I meant. But it was what had come out. The cat was out of the bag, the hen from the hen house. I had revealed how I felt from the way she treated me.

Rejected.

Another reason I avoid women.

I can't bear rejection.

I'm not an ugly man.

Just a lonely one who is damned uncomfortable revealing his feelings.

"Let go!"

And with that, she snapped me out of my momentary mental imprisonment. I let go.

I didn't hear her go so much as I felt this comet of bundled emotions flying off in every direction, flying away from me.

Hurt. Pain. Love. Hope. Despair, but mostly...

Disappointment.

Otter came over and sat down.

"What's with the cold shoulder, Scotch?"

"I hurt her feelings."

"Why, because she won't sleep with you."

"That too," I lied, not wanting to tell him the real reason.

Then he brightened, getting it. "You jerk!"

He got up and went back to sit between the two Midnights again. They began laughing at what he was telling them, motioning towards me.

Someday I'm going to have to fire that guy. But it's hard to do when you don't have any money to pay your partner, and he does the dirty work for free anyway. And the fact that we live in the same flat. Share pretty much everything we have.

We're like brothers, but better. We got no blood in common to keep us tied to each other—just our friendship.

He gave me a look when I got up, slapped a ten down on the tabletop, and stormed for the exit myself.

Again, I didn't see it, so much as feel it. Otter is one of the strongest emotional blasters I know. Besides those that murder or make love.

Both types emit emotion that's so strong I sometimes get ill.

"I'm such a Beagle sometimes," I cursed at myself. And that's one emotion I knew for certain. I'd blurted out my feelings, and then acted like a jerk when I got rejected.

Reminder.

Keep your mouth shut.

Don't look them in the eyes.

Too dangerous, Scotch!

Not meaning I looked like someone you could peg as a jerk. I've actually been told I'm ruggedly handsome and adorable at my best, lovable at my worst. Usually, but tonight I felt horrible because I had hurt Pearl. The one-woman that meant anything to me in this life.

Maybe even the next.

I don't believe in one life.

I believe, however, sometimes we only have one chance.

One chance to make things right.

To do the right thing.

Otter checked me out and nodded as I exited. He knew me too well. I would walk about two miles one way, then two the other, then head for our flat where I would load the juicer with fruits and vegetables, then add some deadly sugar ice cream and fill up.

The double doors to Joe's Bar and Grill swung open for me magically and shut behind me, cutting off the smoke and smell of tobacco that was endemic to bars, even in these modern times.

I stuck my hands into my trench coat, checked the sidewalk before me for any unusual shadows…muggers. Then began hiking my first lap home.

Oh, I forgot to tell you.

It's not just muggers you got to be leery of here in modern London.

Some new kinds of creepos have swung into our fair city to haunt the night and the alleys.

Just pray you never run into them. I have.

They're not a pretty sight!

PEARL ON THE RUN

Pearl cursed herself for being so pig-headed and running off like she had. She was finally used to the fact that Scotch was the first real man she had ever met. No demands. No needs, except the normal ones, which he never pushed on anyone, especially her.

Sometimes she wished he would. Then her habits could kick in, and they'd have a roaring night of pleasure, screams, and groans. But he didn't. And she didn't. Least not with him.

She looked at the pavement, ignoring her surroundings.

Never a wise thing to do this time of the night.

But she was upset.

She really thought she had stirred something in him this time. That he would finally admit, he had…

She wiped at her cheeks, unable to say the same word to herself that she wished he would to her, "I care for you!"

A soft tapping came suddenly to her hearing. She then realized she had heard that sound, steady and unrelenting, following her own steps, since she left the pub. That it hadn't gotten less, but closer, louder.

They weren't soft steps. But loud. Steady.

Like that made by a person who was so sure of themselves, they had no worry or need to disguise or hide what they were, what they planned.

Was he looking for a Midnight Ranger?

Or...

She shook her head.

She was almost to her regular spot.

There would be others there to surround her with support.

She turned the corner, eager to be with them, but instead of rushing forward to chat with her friends, to seek the comfort of their presence, she froze. Unable to step closer.

Four bodies lay on the sidewalk and the street.

Only, they weren't whole.

They were...

Something made a

sudden, swift bite on her neck, causing her to instinctively to swat it. But, as she moved to do so, she found herself unable to make a sound. Her lifeless body joined that of the others on the pavement, falling into pieces as strike after strike of cold, razor-sharp metal struck her even as she tumbled lifeless and loveless forever to the cold, dark, damp pavement.

Scotch was half asleep in his booth when he felt this electric shock burn through his entire body. Startled, he looked about.

For a brief moment, he thought he could see someone he knew.

Someone he cared deeply for. Except she was smiling. Happy and…

"No!" He cried out. He felt as if his heart had been punctured by the sharpest knife that was ever made. His eyes became swollen with tears of grief and regret. But for what? For what?

He woke up from the fatigue that had overcome him and heard Otter's voice hollering for him as he ran into the pub. "Scotch!"

He gave his friend a smile. "What's gotten your guts in such a clench?"

Otter didn't reply.

Scotch felt his waking dream slipping away like an elusive ghost. He could no longer hold onto it, strip it of detail, and analyze it like he always did everything in his profession. But as his vision cleared a bit of fatigue and sleep, he took a closer look at his friend's face then and saw the tears, the hurt, the pain, the great sense of loss.

"No," Scotch uttered.

Otter didn't deny anything. There was nothing to deny.

He just stood there, his eyes watering, doing his best to stop blubbering like an idiot.

Scotch felt this huge pain in his hear then.

"No," he moaned. "Pearl!'

That was when Otter could no longer hold it back. He began blubbering like an idiot, tears sweeping down his cheeks like a dam had burst and released its treasures to the far side.

"No!" Scotch moaned, and then he burst from inside the booth and rushed past Otter.

Scotch and Otter stood side by side as a coffin was slowly lowered into a simple grave. Nothing fancy. No one had the money for more.

As God is my witness, Scotch thought to himself. I am not going to let Pearl or any of her friends be shoved into a cheap folder and forgotten like so many other poor souls have. Lost forever. To justice and love.

Having reached the bottom, the Minister turned to Scotch. "Any last words?"

Scotch looked behind him.

At least several dozen Midnight Rangers were arrayed behind him and Otter. There wasn't a single dry eye amongst the lot of them, and all had a dreadful expression.

He knew that look because he wore it as well.

Anger.

Frustration.

Fear.

He wanted so badly to comfort them. To say they would be all right. But he couldn't promise that.

Could he?

And at that moment, he wept as well. For Pearl, for her lost friends, for the others like her, that might soon join...for himself.

Now, he had to face a part of his life he had kept buried for years now. He had refused to acknowledge

or give any thought to because of the grief he felt for the loss of his father.

"Father!" He whispered forlornly.

He wept then.

And as he did, he clenched his hands into fists. Because with the grief came a storm of anger. A need to make things right.

To bring justice to the fallen.

"I'm not giving you this case, Scotch, you're too close to it," Inspector Dublin replied, wiping at his pale face. He hadn't slept in days, maybe even weeks.

Everyone knew he lived and breathed his work. He didn't even have a wife or children. *No time for them,* he would say.

But tonight.

It was after Midnight.

The cock had crowed a long, long time ago, and even Dracula, if he was alive and real...even he would be hard put to think of staying awake much longer. The dawn was already pinking the skies outside the Inspectors office window, delicately scribing the morning clouds ad skies with traces of soft daisy pink, dispelling the deep lavender and stark royal blues of the night.

"All right, you won't," Scotch finally replied.

He was determined to solve this case, even if there was nothing in it for him.

Otter was seated next to him, still a wreck from earlier. His expression was lifeless. His own grief fueled despair, not unlike that of Scotch. But Scotch knew why.

Pearl was the only woman who treated his peculiar friend with any level of respect and kindness. His cross-eyes and balding hair repelled most women. True, he was muscular and quite strong. But first appearances counted for a lot…even for a man who dressed quite respectably as Otter did.

The Inspector stood up. His lanky shape barely grazed his desk's right edge as he came around to confront Scotch. "I mean it."

"And I do," Scotch replied, fingers crossed behind his back.

"Do what?"

"What you said," Scotch told the Inspector with a straight face, keeping his fingers tightly crossed behind his back.

"I don't trust you, Scotch."

"Have I ever lied to you, Inspector?"

The Inspector swept his green eyes to the left and shook his head. "But you always find a way around your promises, don't you?"

"Ask no promises, and I'll try no lies," Scotch quoted an old saying.

"You can't even get that straight," the Inspector replied with a hint of amusement.

Otter was finally coming out of his funk. And when he saw Scotch's crossed fingers, he began to giggle.

The Inspector whipped around.

"Now get out, I've got work to do."

Otter and Scotch rose to leave.

The Inspector reached over and put a hand on both men's shoulders, causing them to pause at the exit doorway.

"For what it's worth…"

Scotch nodded. "Thanks."

Otter began blubbering again.

ANGEL FLATS

Angel Flats is a relatively new building built from an older series of flats that fronted Baker Street.

Scotch had affection for the old Doyle stories and his cold detective, who always solved his crimes, and so had sought refuge in the closest thing he could to the reality of that Holmesian world.

But instead of 221B Baker Street, it was 221B Angel Flats on Baker Street.

He had even once toyed with trying to get the flats renamed, but he didn't have enough money or position in the London circles of power to do that.

Yet.

Scotch and Otter climbed out of their old beat-up Bentley. At least, it looked beat up; it wasn't. It had a souped-up electric engine, its paint job was solar paint that collected power to run all the electricity the engine and the interior needed, as well as their mag headlights and tail lights.

It had cost him his inheritance to do it.

It had cost him even more than that to accept the inheritance. It was another who had needed him, and he wasn't there to save them.

His father.

Close for years as a child, but further and further alienated as a growing young man, he had been estranged from him until his mother died, and then his father had suddenly opened up to him.

When it was too late to make a difference in their relationship, he thought, regret surging in a torrent of self-pity for a moment. Scotch, all his life, had wished for a closer relationship with his father. Now, it was closed to him. A dream that was lost in the swirling channels of time forever.

Cancer.

"Son," Able McBride had whispered.

It was the best he could do.

And even then, his whole body would contort with pain. He was being eaten up from the inside out. The cancer had spread to every major organ.

Scotch, when he found out, had insisted on putting his father in the best of hospitals.

"No!"

Scotch hadn't done it.

The no was final, and he knew it.

"I must have something left I can bequeath you once I am..."

"No, father, don't..."

His father had clenched his arm hard then. But he wasn't angry; he was smiling. This had to have hurt a lot and taken a lot of his precious energy left to do. But he had smiled and for the first time in years.

"I love you, Scotch McBride. You've done me proud. I only wish..."

His father's hand slipped from Scotch's arm, and his father's head tilted to the right.

BIG BOOM

"The Big Boom!" She said with a shiver.

Scotch sat on the loveseat facing her. She was seated at a large octagonal shaped table of highly polished walnut wood with a white linen circle of cloth at its center, topped by a beautiful stained glass candlestick holder with eight candles burning, casting flickering shadows about the room.

"What big boom?"

She played with an earlobe a moment, causing the tiny silver bells of the earring there to tinkle sweetly. He always enjoyed that part about her.

She was huge for a woman. Fat, some would say, but to him, she was none of those things. She was even loud and bellicose at times, belched and farted loud enough to rival most men, but he never felt offended. She was as natural with that as she was with all the things in her world.

She was almost angelic if angels could be said to fart and belch. He hoped they could; otherwise, Heaven must be a dreadfully, dull place if everything were always perfectly the same.

She gave him one of her usual smiles. The kind that melted your heart and made you want to call her mother like he had never called his own. "Scotchie, you're the most desirable man. Why haven't you married yet?"

He avoided the question. "What Big Boom?"

She ignored his diversion and cut to the chase. "Because you are more interested in facts than figures."

She burst into laughter.

"Got me," he uttered and laughed with her.

Her jokes were very unlike most women he knew and always got to the part of him that needed the most...his heart.

She was heart food for his soul.

If angels could do the things Pearl could live on earth, then Heaven was definitely a place he would want to be. Just not yet.

She shuffled the cards before her and began dealing them out. "Join me, Scotchie."

He got up and sat opposite her.

She smiled as she finished dealing the cards.

"In my last life, I used to be a medium and would oftentimes tell gamblers how to win or lose."

"Lose?"

She gave him that winning grin that always lit up his heart and her face. "It's not always about winning, Scotch. Sometimes losing can be as important and life-changing as winning."

He nodded and then grinned. "So, what is the Big Boom?"

She burst into laughter.

That was the way of Madame Crystal. And I would have her no other way than that.

Thank the gods and God for a woman of such a big heart and even bigger understanding.

CLUES AND DEAD ENDS

Otter grimaced as the body...or rather the remains of Pearl...were drawn from a cool drawer used to preserve the body and keep it from corrupting too fast.

Scotch grimaced inside.

"This the woman named Pearl Morning?"

Scotch nodded. "But sometimes she'd call herself Morning Star."

The M.E., Medical Examiner, pulled the sheet back over her body and rolled her drawer back inside the refrigerator.

He made some notes on his form and then gave Otter a sympathetic look. "Your girlfriend?"

Otter really began to bawl then.

Scotch took a few moments to guide his friend back into the conference room. There, Inspector Dublin waited. Scotch gave the Inspector a nod, then returned to the Cold Room...which was what the constables called the morgue.

"What have you got for me, Doctor?" He asked the Medical Examiner.

The man swept a hand through his thinning hair and then frowned.

"The lacerations were evidently made by a superbly crafted blade."

"Oh?"

"Yes," the Doctor said, his expression growing quite grim. "Impossibly crafted."

"What do you mean?"

The Doctor looked away.

"I need to know."

The Doctor looked at Scotch, searching his face. "I don't know how much of a clue this is for you, detective, but no weapon on earth is capable of cutting a human body that perfectly."

"No weapon," Scotch asked. "Or no blade?"

The Doctor didn't reply.

YE OLDE WEAPONS SHOP

"Marlin!" I greeted.

Marlin kept his head down; he was oiling an old McGruder bore and twist. One of those ancient rifles that held an odd number of huge caliber bullets that can punch a hole in a man's chest wide enough for an elephant to dance through.

It more closely resembled a portable cannon than an actual rifle. It had been designed and invented by Horace McGruder. A famous Scot, who dabbled in the art of weaponry, with an emphasis on exotic weapons. This was precisely why he chose Marlin's shop as the first port of call.

If anyone might know that exotic weapon he was looking at, he suspected it would be he.

"Scotch!"

I glided about the tiny shop, my hands barely touching on a Japanese ceremonial sword. It was carefully sheathed. I knew how sharp that blade was. Enough to slice a man's head off with barely a move. But not the weapon that had killed those poor Midnight Rangers. That had been some kind of remote device. Otherwise, the lot of them could never have been quartered so mercilessly, so violently. So frequently that none had a chance to escape or scream for help.

The evening sun was long gone.

The moon was silvering the pavement and car tops outside.

A couple pigeons landed on the one outside and perched them, pecking at each other in that kissy-kissy kind of way that birds do.

For a moment, I felt sad. I suppose if I had taken the time, I would've realized it was because of Pearl.

I sniffed my nose a couple of times, swiped at my eyes with the cuff of my right trench coat sleeve, then waited for Marlin to finish.

"Sorry."

I gave him a surprised look.

He finished and looked up at me, but I was already staring at his shirt collar, checking it out.

He smiled.

I didn't' see it; I can always tell by the way a person shuffles or positions themselves differently when they're smiling. It's an innate intuitive type of thing I do. Well. Very, very well.

"About?"

Marlin laid the McGruder down on his narrow glass counter, got up from the stool he had sat on, went to the front door, locked it, and then pulled the steel blinds down that kept anyone from breaking in.

You'd be surprised how many blighters love to get their hands on the big bore guns.

He eyed me uncertainly. "You never visit much anymore."

"I know. Sorry. I live on the other side of town now."

He nodded and sat opposite me again.

He reached beneath his counter where he kept his coffee warmer, brought up a small glass urn half-filled with brew, then two mugs and filled them both. He plopped sugar in both of them, then a lemon slice in mine, and handed me that one.

I sipped it. Made a face.

He did too. "I don't know how you handle all that lemon in your coffee, Scotch."

"Me, either."

Time to warm him up for my question.

"So, how is business this week?"

It was Friday. He'd had five days now to drum up a few quid to tide him over.

He nodded absentmindedly over his own coffee and then sighed. "Lousy."

"Oh?"

He looked up, and I quickly averted my eyes. Almost got me. They try to do that sometimes, but I'm quicker.

"Yeah. The only sale was to some scumbag who wanted a heavy caliber submachine gun."

"You sold him one?"

He shook his head. "Nah. You know I'm not licensed for that. And even if I could get one, I'd never do it. Too many tykes being rubbed out by those things over in the colonies."

I chuckled.

He grinned. It was an inside joke. America was still officially in many of our minds, just a colony. A very arrogant and silly one at times because of their politics, but we still loved her.

"I understand."

"Suppose you do," he replied, adding nothing more.

He had more.

"Marlin, you're holding out on me!"

He sighed and sipped his coffee a long time, gathering his thoughts, and then he set his mug down, fondled it between his hands, and said...

A POUND OF NOTHING

I eyed the building warily.

"Otter, take the back. Don't do anything stupid."

Otter gave me a look. "Really? Me? What about you? You brought a stinking Muff with you!"

I looked down at Muff. He had refused to leave me when I left earlier. The silly thing had rushed between my legs, dodging both Otter and me from catching him. When we got into our old Bentley, hoping he would abandon us and stick, he didn't. He yelped like a puppy and ran after us.

Otter was forced to stop the car for fear of running over the poor thing. With a sigh like a man who is totally tormented and martyred, Otter got out, opened the back door. Muff jumped in, but instead of staying there, leaped over the front seat and into my lap.

As Otter climbed inside, he barked at Otter.

"See, now I'm where I should be," it told him.

Otter shook his head and put the car in gear again. "I knew he was smiling then, but he hid it so I couldn't see, but Muff knew best. He began wagging his tail vigorously and climbed between the two of us and snuggled down.

Argument over.

Dog wins.

"Weird name for a business," Otter muttered as he girded himself with his usual assortment of weapons. A fork, a knife, and a spoon.

You might laugh at him for doing that, but believe me, he's dangerous with those. Very, very dangerous.

He skirted the side of the car and headed across the street for the alley that sided the building, keeping to the shadows.

I climbed from my side. Muff leaped from my lap and landed on the sidewalk. He immediately went to the rear car wheel and raised a leg to mark his territory.

"Muff!" I hissed.

Too late.

Otter was really, really going to hate my new friend.

I sighed, and then adjusted my coat, checking to make sure my weapon was safely holstered. It was I sauntered away from the car, not heading across the street like Otter had at an angle, but up the street until the building was no longer in eye range.

The evening moon cast the majority of the buildings in this warehouse district in heavy shadows. I found one that crossed the street and entered it.

BACKWAYS

"How do we know Marlin's client is the one?" Otter asked as we entered the back door.

Otter stepped aside for me to enter in front of him. The back door was slightly off its hinges. He tucked his fork away, then his knife and spoon after straightening their handles then followed me inside.

"Gotta start somewhere, me lad," I consoled him. Not sure myself, but I put a lot of trust in my hunches. They're usually quite educated.

We were looking for a man who was good with weapons. Exotic weapons. Who loved guns, but loved sharp edges even more.

Clive Burkhardt fits the bill.

Perfectly.

And if not, maybe he knew someone, who knew someone, who...

Well, you get the point.

Something warm and fuzzy glanced between our legs and rushed ahead, tongue hanging out happily. Least I imagined so, as most of the moonlight didn't go so far as we had gone already.

But dogs are guided by more than their eyes. And Muff as no exception.

For Muff, this was just a fun game. Or one might think so by how eager the critter was. But I'm not one to judge harshly without proper reason. I just hope I wasn't putting my new friend into danger. I hoped I hadn't made a mistake bringing him.

But he didn't bark. And to me, that was nothing short of a miracle, but he did scent. He seemed to be on some kind of trail, with his nose down to the floor, the tail now shot straight behind him, and so I moved further to my right. There, two sets of stairs curved upwards. Muff's shadowy form was at the left one. He began wagging his tail vigorously, then looked back at me and nodded his head.

Otter whispered. "This dog freaks me out."

Could Muff have supernatural powers of observation as well as doggie power? A question I couldn't answer at that time, but certainly might explain some of his most...and I emphasize most, most sincerely...inexplicable actions.

To me, at the time.

"Me too," I finally answered Otter, but I took the direction Muff had taken anyway.

Otter and I moved very quietly.

If my hunch was right, we needed to be more careful than usual.

And it was.

Muff barked from ahead of us and leaped past us downwards.

I pulled Otter down.

Swish!

A blade whizzed overhead and slammed into the sidewall. It crunched deeply, slicing through drywall and wood paneling.

That was the only other sound for a long moment.

When Otter and I could breathe again, Muff was back between our legs, but this time, not leading.

I dropped to a knee and petted him. "Good boy!"

Muff wasn't buying it. He let out a low whine and then dropped so low to the floor, I thought he was about to become one with it.

The hair rose on the back of my neck.

"Down!" I shouted.

Swish.

Otter and I hit the floor again as a second blade whizzed through space we had been and smashed into the wall beside the back door.

"See him?"

"No blast it all anyway!" I cursed.

But Muff knew where he was.

And went the opposite way. Even a dog as canny or uncanny as this one was, knew its boundaries.

I jerked Otter by his right arm and began crawling as fast as I could back the way we had come. Muff wasn't far behind. In fact, he was ahead of us.

We were just about to the back door when it slammed shut and what little light there had been was snuffed out, just like our lives were about to be cut short as well.

TRAPS AND VILLAINS

We both lay there like trapped rats in a deadly maze with no way out and a very real chance of getting our better senses severed from our lesser ones.

"Stop licking my face!"

"I didn't," I responded in a hiss.

"Then stop it anyway!" Otter insisted.

Then I smelled Muff's doggy breath in my face, and he began licking on me.

We both heard the sound of feet trampling hard down the stairs, then run, but not towards us.

Muff began barking immediately and ran off.

"Damn, dog's gonna get us killed!" Otter swore then was up on his feet with his fork and spoon out.

I jumped to mine, and we ran after the one we had been seeking. My suspicions had proven true.

Clive Burkhardt lived here or, rather, worked here, from what his Boss had told us over the telly.

***

"This fellow is a bit on the eccentric side."

"How much?" I asked.

"Do you ever watch the reruns of X-Files?"

"Sometimes."

"That strange. That...weird."

"Oh," I replied.

***

End of conversation as far as I was concerned.

Clive was a loner. Had been to Marlin's shop and was a bit psychotic, obviously. As only men with a love of death more than life frequented Marlin's shop.

Which might seem odd, my saying that. But Marlin is a craftsman who truly has a great heart and love of weaponry. Many others are fascinated. But the ones who purchase from Clive tend to be the odd sort. Not necessarily violent or crazy, but with a touch of psychotic nature, most of us would not embrace, even on one of our darker nights.

So...the blades pretty much put a punctuation point to my hunch that Clive was the villain we were after. And with that came a sense of relief. And a deepening sense of grief as images of my lost Pearl ate at the back of my mind and dug deeply into my aching heart.

I didn't want to admit it at the moment, but every time I saw a woman resembling Pearl after that, I would feel my heart leap for joy. She wasn't dead. She couldn't be. There she was. And then the woman would turn her face to look at me, sensing my desperate need to affirm what I felt, and I would be crushed yet again.

How long does it take to get over such grief?

I don't know.

I'll tell you when it happens.

***

We burst from the back room, ran through the clothing racks that bound both sides of the aisle we ran down.

Ahead of us, Muff was faster.

He caught up with the running person.

They tripped and fell.

Muff got to biting.

A curse of pain exploded.

A woman's.

I took out my mag-lite the same time as Otter, and we nailed the figure on the floor. Muff was no longer biting. He was licking the face of the woman lying there on the floor. She looked really, really mad!

"Will you blokes turn those damned lights off. You're blinding me."

We did.

"Nice doggie. What a sweet thing you are?"

The thumping of Muff's tail announced his response.

I can't tell you why, but something about the way she said *nice doggie* and he thumped his tail didn't bode well.

CONFESSIONS OF A SOBBY SORT

McDonald's, God bless them, sometimes comes in handy. This was one of those times. The hour was late, and none of us had the time or the energy to seek a fancy restaurant. Not to mention I hadn't had time to cash that lovely little check yet.

Otter was seated to her left, and me her right. Muff sat on the tabletop, employees glaring at him, but him daring them to object, his ears up flat to his skull, and snarling if they so much as approached the table.

I suspected trouble, so I flashed them my detective badge, and they backed off, giving Muff the evil eye as they did so.

Muff ignored them and fixed the woman with his big brown doggie eyes again as if weighing whether to bite her now or later.

She eyed him back. "You bite me; you lick me; now you wanna bite me again? Men! Sheesh!"

Muff's ears perked up straight, and he began wagging his tail as she laid a strip of bacon in front of him.

He ate it and then looked up again. She laughed.

"Okay, enough dog play," Otter finally said, yawning big. "It's late. Fess up."

"Nothing to fess too," she said, finishing her Big Mac Bacon Chicken sandwich."

She sipped at her coke and then rocked back on her chair to eye the two of us.

"You two are an odd couple."

"Not a couple," Otter protested immediately.

She laughed. "Sure, you're not."

Before Otter could explode, I put a hand up. "Why were you there?"

She slipped a hand between her breasts.

Otter and I both scrambled for our weapons.

She held a hand up to stop us. "Please!"

We hesitated, and she slowly withdrew a legal looking document. "I was serving."

I flipped it over and read it. "You were trying to serve divorce papers?"

"Sure. It's a job, and the jerk had it coming to him. Cut up all her dolls and furniture before he split."

Otter and I exchanged glances.

"How?" I asked.

"The guy's some kind of nutso inventor or something."

Otter and I glanced at each other again.

I got up.

Otter got up.

"Where you two going?"

"Home. To sleep," Otter replied testily.

He walked off, Muff dogging his heels.

I yawned. "Thanks for the intel."

"Look, Mister Scotchbright."

"Scotch McBride," I corrected her.

She blushed a moment, heavily, then said, "I have a stake in this too. If you're going after him, I wanna be there. My rent's hanging on getting him served."

I eyed her sternly. "Lady…"

"Patricia. Patricia Bell."

"Patricia," I said in my kindest voice. "This man is a deranged serial killer. I don't think he's going to wait around for you to serve him."

She reached into her blouse again.

This time she pulled out a small derringer.

On my look, she grinned and then gave me a big wink.

I grinned back at her.

Another big mistake.

Muff barked and thumped his tail.

Big trouble was coming.

And it wasn't just the dog now.

221 B ANGEL FLATS ON BAKER STREET

She wouldn't let go of me. Not for a damned moment. She kept talking all the way to our flat. I've never met a more determined woman in my life than this, Patricia Bell. She frightened me. Absolutely frightened me.

And of course, I couldn't admit that to her. That would be telling now, wouldn't it? And it's never good to be impolite to a lady.

She spits on the pavement as she got out of our Bentley and eyed our building.

"You two don't make much, do you?"

Otter was about to explode. I shook my head.

She stormed ahead of us, following Muff, who ripped up the stairs to start barking at the front door.

I glanced at Otter.

He said, "First, we got owned by Muff; now a woman?"

We had to admit it then. We had been outsmarted by both a dog and a woman. Anyone that says it's a man's world has never met our dog and this woman.

We both headed for the steps to see if we could somehow find some peace of mind, and hopefully, a few hours of sleep before this night were finished.

Wasn't going to happen.

I gawked at her face, not believing what she had just told me.

Otter believed her. He believed every single word so much that he had lost consciousness several hours ago as she rambled on and on and on.

Finally, she took a breath.

"All this time?"

"All of it!"

Now I knew why Muff liked her. Not only was she quick on her feet. After all, she could've lost her head, but she didn't. But she knew how to tell a story. On and on and on.

And I have to admit, she didn't hold back any punches. Not a woman to get mad at you. Not if you don't want all your dirty little secrets shared.

I scratched at my beard.

"You don't shave either?"

I gave her a blank look.

She looked about Otter and my living room. "Looks like a tornado struck...months ago. Your kitchen has dishes piled several stories high, your trash hasn't been taken out for weeks..."

I held up a hand.

"Look, you're a guest at the moment, don't push it."

She finally stopped talking and gave me the most forlorn look I have ever seen.

Even Muff, who had been napping intermittently, woke up, sensing her distress. He made a sad sound and dropped his head onto his paws, giving us those big brown sad eyes.

"I have nowhere to go."

"But you said you've been living in the warehouse…"

"I lied."

"You lied? Why?"

She wiped at a tear forming in her right eye. "I'm a total failure. I can't even afford rent. If my employer knew I had been hiding out after work so I could sleep there, I wouldn't even have a job and enough to buy meals."

She looked at me, trying to see me in my eyes. But not a chance of that. I averted my head as usual and eyed her neck. "What do you want?"

She put a handout. It was firm and warm. She gripped my arm and squeezed. "You're a good man, Scotch McBride, and even your gruff friend."

Otter began making mumbling sounds in his sleep.

"I need a place to stay. I noticed when we entered, you have three bedrooms."

"I use the third to do my meditations."

"I'd be willing to share it."

I gave her a surprised look. "Share…"

She gave me a look just like Muff was at that moment. "Please. I'm a nice person. I'll make sure your house looks like a million dollars. And if you want, I'll even ride shotgun for you."

I gave her a new surprised look. At her neck, of course.

"I…"

She squeezed harder.

"Please!"

Muff made whining sounds like he was ready to burst into tears.

Otter mumbled in his sleep again.

This time I did look her in the eyes.

Big mistake.

Then she said, "My name's Pearl. Pearl Anderson."

Inspector Dublin stood to my right, watching his forensics team go about their job from one end of the warehouse to the other.

"And you say you were here to serve him?" Inspector Dublin asked Pearl, who stood to my right, still wearing the same dress as last night, but somehow cleaner and smelling good.

"I was."

He looked at me. "You believe her?"

I handed him the paperwork. He eyed it quickly, then nodded and handed it back towards me. She snatched it and shoved it back between her breasts, giving me a smile that dared me to take it back.

The Inspector sighed. "Well, good enough, then. But are you sure this man was the one you were serving?"

She winked at the Inspector, catching him both off guard and now shocking him. "Do I look like the sort of woman who jokes about such things?"

Unable to come back with a proper response, the Inspector marched off to holler at one of his men.

"He's a tough sort, that man," she admitted.

I smiled.

She didn't know how much. But I was beginning to suspect this woman wouldn't take very long to find out.

"Show me where you slept," I asked her.

She led the way through lines of crates and up the stairs to the right. We reached the top, and she was about to reach into her bosom again.

I stopped her with a shake of my head.

I reached for the door she had indicated and tried its knob. Click. It was open.

She gave me a surprised look. "I didn't leave it unlocked. "

"Maybe you forget in your rush to get away."

"Not fat likely," she shot back, annoyed at my even suggesting such a thing.

I reached into my jacket and came out with baseball.

"A baseball? You expect to stop a bullet with that?"

I grinned.

"No, I intend to stop us from stopping a bullet with this baseball."

I gently opened the door and then hurled the baseball inside.

I heard it crash against a wall, then bounce several times.

Nothing!

I frowned.

"Maybe you did leave it unlocked."

I was about to open the door further when a sword slashed through space where my hand and arm would've been.

A SLICE OF FREEDOM

Pearl let out a shriek that matched my own as I fell back against her.

She grabbed me hard to keep me from stumbling over her when I hurriedly backed up. We stared at the open space where the blade struck the floor and was still vibrating from the force of its impact.

"Thanks!"

She nodded.

I gently opened the door with my foot. Better my toe than my fingers, I thought. I was so rattled that I had forgotten I could just as easily have used my trusty old 40 calibers Smith and Wesson semi-automatic.

I keep it tucked over my right side in a left-hander holster, with extra clips fitted to the holster bands. Never know when you might get invited to a party, you know.

Nothing further happened.

This time I pulled out my Smith and Wesson, letting it lead the way inside after I kicked the door open the rest of the way, in case someone thought they could hide behind it.

They weren't.

The door slammed into the wall and rebounded from my foot, which felt safe enough to stab into the empty space now.

Pearl blanched.

"Oh, Christ, Mary!" She swore, calling on two names that seemed comfortable in her mouth.

Better than what usually came out of Otter's mouth and mine sometimes. Not that I swear often, or even loudly. But a banged head or foot, or such warrants at least a cursory curse upon one's lips.

Pearl's office space was fourteen by fourteen with two windows on the outside, heavily blinded now, four walls that had once been covered with beautiful posters of artists she loved and a few musical artists, which I don't.

But whatever peace and calm there had been here was now gone. The office space she worked in was a shambles. Everything was cut to ribbons. Even the walls had huge slices in them.

She dropped to her knees and lifted the bodiless head of John Lennon, one of the few musicians I adored, and kissed the top of his ragamuffin's hair. The rest was gone, except for his glasses and chin.

"Oh, Johnnie boy," she began to sing.

Inspector Dublin and several constables rushed inside, weapons out.

"You two all right?"

I half bowed to him, giving him my usual dimpled smile. "Well, and if it is well ye be looking for, then I'm afraid dear darling Pearl here is far from that spot of rainbow t the moment."

"Evidently, our slicer has a mad-on for posters."

Pearl looked up. "He even ruined my Beatles posters. I bought them at an auction. They were worth hundreds for each of them. It was my retirement money."

Her beautiful eyes began to water, then she made muffled sobs in her throat, trying not to be obnoxious to him. But it wasn't to him. He cared. He gave her a comforting hand on her shoulder. "There, there now, Pearl. I'm sure we can rustle up more posters for you from somewhere."

"I don't have that kind of money anymore," she said, then emitted a heartbreaking moan I will never forget.

The Inspector rolled his eyes theatrically. He did his best to look like the official he was supposed to be, not the profoundly disturbed human being he was by this woman's cry of pain. He spun about and ordered his men, "Fetch the forensics team and have them go over this entire room for fingerprints and anything else with possible clues."

I helped Pearl get back to her feet, and led her downstairs, a grieving woman, with no home to stay and no life to look back upon.

She leaned hard against me.

I don't usually do leaning, but I figured she was half out of her mind with grief.

Strange world, isn't it?

"My Bonnie lies over the ocean, my Bonnie lies over the sea…" Pearl sang from our kitchen.

Otter and I both sat petrified in the living room. The TV was on, and BBC blared the latest nonsense about America and its politics, God help those poor souls there. And of course, about the Russians and their usual shenanigans, Putin created to shake up the world. Last came more enlightening news. The rise of a new dictator and thousands of innocent lives slaughtered as he rose to power.

Our world never gets a dull moment, does it?"

Otter snorted and then looked from the TV. Barbara Hirsch, an older stage actress, was playing a detective, called "Madam Chuckles."

I laughed. Missus Hirsh was a bad actress, but I had to admit she did the chuckling part quite well, especially when the criminals were caught with their pants down. Quite Literally. I could see their blushing bottoms!

Evidently, the BBC thought viewers needed a bit more aggressive female detective than their favorite Sherlock Holmes. A detective who wasn't afraid of dressing down a man… mostly if he was a criminal.

The man was also a bodybuilder with enormous biceps. His Adonis's face told me he was shooting for ratings to sell the show. Not here. No one cares. But, overseas...probably to the Americans who seemed to be hung on sex and violence at the moment.

Me, give me my Benny Hill and the old Laurel and Hardy comedies. I don't hate a good show with sex or violence; just think it gets to be a bit like masturbation after a while. Lots of it that goes nowhere. An orchestra without players.

I laughed at my own joke.

Otter glanced at me.

"Not funny."

Madame Chuckles had just pantsed a man. Several constables had rushed in with nightsticks out to bash him over the head if he moved.

"Wasn't laughing at the good Madame, Otter."

"Oh." He glanced at me. "Then what were you laughing at?"

"Dinner's ready!" Pearl called to us.

She came into the living room where our dining table was and set down a huge platter.

I think Otter and I both fell in love immediately with her at that moment. The most heavenly scents were rising from the huge platter. On it sat an assortment of fresh slices of bread, minted potatoes, a pot of the size of a good soup bowl with Irish stew, fresh coffee, and tea were arrayed.

We quickly got up and helped her set the table with plates and utensils.

Needless to say, we didn't go to bed unhappy that night. As a matter of fact, we both had to let our belts out, we ate so much.

As for Pearl, she had sealed her birth in our home at the small cost of a good meal.

The rest is history.

TO SLEEP, TO SLEEP, PERCHANCE TO...

I sat on the edge of the nicely trimmed mound of lawn that fronted George O'Hara's mansion on Trillion Street. The whole street is an exercise in excess wealth. Not a home there is worth less than ten million pounds. All their rooftops are guaranteed to touch the blue skies. Each one decorated with snarling, laughing or solemn gnomes, attached to teepee shaped gables.

It's a treasure for tourists sightseeing. And a payday for the tourist industry, whose buses frequented the more popular areas of London.

I could hear the Tourist Guide now as the bus turned onto Trillion Street and slowed. "And here we have George O'Hara's mansion. Once an employee of the late and great Walt Disney, he is now happily retired at the ripe old age of 93."

Ripe. Now that's a conundrum if ever I heard one.

"And if you look on his front lawn near the vaulted gate entrance, you will see Snow White and Grumpy dancing on a pedestal made of pure white marble."

Imported from Italy, no doubt.

I frowned.

What in the world was I doing on Trillion Street? Mimicking a Tourist Guide, when I should be sound asleep on my bed. Pondering the slice murderer, his motives, his victims, and, more importantly, where he might strike next.

For a brief moment, I saw my right hand and foot sliced off and lying in a mangled pool of flesh and blood, then I saw my own head, cocked at its usual humble angle, but on the ground.

My eyes were wide open.

The usual grin lit my lips.

But I did not like the look of it.

A headless detective has much to lose and little to gain in the professional world.

And with that thought, my dream shattered, along with the sound of a dish.

I shrugged on my night robe and slippers, and then rushed into the kitchen.

Pearl was standing there looking at the mess she had made.

"I'm so sorry!" She sobbed.

I touched her right arm lightly and pressed it gently. "Accidents happen."

"This wasn't an accident. "

I gave her a sharp look.

She wiped at her eyes.

"I saw something."

"Something, as in what?"

She went to our window and pulled the curtains way to reveal a sky full of stars.

"A face. Right here. Looking in at me."

I looked out.

We were three stories up. Fat likely of any chance burglar or night intruder being that high off the ground. Unless he could fly like the legendary Peter pan, that is.

I turned about and examined her.

"Pearl, have you been drinking something besides tea or coffee?"

With that statement, she burst into more tears. Then she rushed from the kitchen, slamming the door to our guest room.

Otter came into the kitchen a moment later, rubbing his eyes. He saw the broken glass. "Since when did you get up in the middle of the night and have coffee?"

"Since, when haven't I?"

He raised his eyebrows in concern.

"It's Pearl; she saw something or someone."

"In here?" Otter asked, peering about the semi-lit kitchen as if suspecting someone or something to suddenly leap from the shadowed corners and attack us.

I flicked on the electrics, and the kitchen flooded with light.

He frowned. Looked at me. "Where?"

I pointed to the kitchen window.

Otter took a big yawn and then shook his head. "Women!"

He pulled his night robe tighter about him, and tread back to his room and shut the door.

Now it was my turn to frown.

If I couldn't sleep before. Now I most certainly wouldn't be doing any sleeping. Added to that, we now had a dangerous splash of porcelain bits on the kitchen floor.

I sighed, went to the closet, and hiked out the swift broom, a short one for just this kind of thing, dragged the garbage can from beneath the sink over, and then began brushing the pieces up over its lip and inside.

Good thing it was empty was the only thought on my mind. Which, if you know me...can only mean one thing.

MORNING AFTER BLUES AND GREENS

"Celery?"

"Yup!"

"For breakfast?"

"What better time?"

I nodded.

I heard the scud of the morning paper on our front porch. Got up from the dining room table, where Otter was eating a bowl of celery for breakfast., then scurried down the flight of stairs to the front door and opened it.

Then I let out a yell loud enough to wake up every neighbor up and down Baker Street and then a few miles more besides.

Inspector Dublin eyed the head lying on the metal gurney, spread nicely upon a fresh white cloth, and a silver bowl next to it for the M.E.

"A head? No body?"

"Seems likely."

"On your front porch?"

"Actually, right above it."

He eyed me with an uncertain frown. "Why would someone dress your porch with a bodiless head?"

"Inspector, you are asking the wrong question?"

"Then what is the right question," he asked, obviously short on patience, and not having eaten breakfast any more than I had.

How could I?

Finding a head dangling in your vision when you open a front door to look out and bumping noses with it are most disconcerting, to say the least.

"Well?" He demanded, stamping his right foot impatiently. A nervous habit of the man, even as mine was to cock my head and wince at times when I got certain revelations. "And stop wincing!" He told me, affirming my habit as still being quite strong and able to provoke others as usual.

I pondered the depth of his question and then said, very cautiously. "Once the M.E. has looked at the head, I shall be more certain."

"Of what?"

"That it's the work of the Slicer."

"Don't you go spilling that world out into the press, Scotch, or I'll have your detective's badge tossed in the Thames and buried under ten tons of cement!"

"A bit of work, isn't it?" I asked cheerily.

"You..." he started, and then caught himself.

Otter rushed into the Cold Room with a late morning paper. "Scotch, you gotta see this headline. It's rip-roaring!"

I took the paper and unfolded it.

"Scotch Mc Bride, an internationally famous detective, stationed here in London, has been threatened by a vicious criminal, recently revealed by the nomer of "The Slicer!"

I looked up.

The Inspector gave us both a low throated growl and then exited the room.

A moment later, Flim O'Brien entered, taking a pull of his pipe as he did so.

He blew out the smoke, spotted the head, and then cocked an eye on it. "On your front porch, no doubt?"

"How did you know that?"

"Heard the local news lad yelling it on the corner. The Inspector is going to roast you for that bit of amusement."

"I didn't do it."

"Doesn't matter. You know how much the Inspector hates publicity."

"Negative publicity."

Flim grinned. "Don't tell the Inspector this, but the lads are preparing a surprise for him to thank him for his years of friendly oversight."

"What would that be?"

Then he told me.

Otter and I both barked with laughter.

THE HEADLESS MYSTERY

Flim stood inside the oval-shaped meeting room. Half a dozen Yard detectives sat about it, along with Inspector Dublin, I and Otter, who was nibbling on another piece of celery.

I wrinkled my nose. "Again?"

"Healthy!" He told me, holding up a piece for me to take.

I shook my head. "I like my veggies in a proper stew."

"Oh, that reminds me. Pearl sent this."

He gave me a scribbled message. I quickly read it. "Sorry for earlier. I asked Otter what kind of meal you prefer for dinner."

I looked up at Otter.

He grinned. "Stew!"

"Stew?" The Inspector asked when his ear became free again.

"Nothing, Inspector," I told him.

He nodded but gave me a suspicious look. What kind of shenanigan was I up to now?

"As we all know by now," Flim spoke up, gathering our attention back to him again."

Once all were quiet, he continued. "...we have a serial killer loose in London."

"A Slicer," one of the detectives spouted up.

"Howard!" The Inspector warned.

"Sorry, just got excited is all."

The Inspector frowned.

"You know, at having the opportunity to protect the community."

The Inspector frowned again.

Howard got up. "I'll get us some coffee."

"Good idea," the Inspector agreed.

Flim spoke up again. "While I would prefer not to offer such an obvious nickname to our killer, it is appropriate to say that is exactly how he murders his victims. Slices them."

The Inspector winced on the word "slices."

Scotch cleared his throat. "Technically, we have to call it beheading."

"Slices," Flim insisted.

The Inspector gave Scotch an appreciative look for a moment, then grumbled. "On with it, Flim, before I have a stroke, and there's the end of it."

Flim laughed, and then he gave the Inspector a closer look. "Sir?"

The Inspector waved his hand at Flim. "Joke."

"Bad one," Scotch pointed out.

This time the Inspector scowled at him.

"The point is, no matter what we technically, or he professionally…, " Slaps a newspaper with its headlines face up before him. "…The end result is the same. We have people dying. And…"

He eyed Scotch a moment. "A detective who has been useful from time to time…"

"Thank you, Inspector, you're a good man," Scotch said with a grin.

"Time to time," the Inspector insisted with a new scowl.

Otter chuckled into his hand.

Scotch raised an eyebrow questioningly.

"The point is, we are dealing with a madman."

"But a smart one," Scotch spoke up again.

To this, the Inspector had no reply.

Scotch rose. "And one who has left us yet another clue."

"Another?" The Inspector inquired, a puzzled tone to his voice. He scratched at his thinning hair a moment and then asked. "What other? What before?"

Scotch eyed Otter, who nodded, then stood. "Being a chemist, sometimes. Sometimes, mind you." Eyeing Scotch sternly. "Comes in handy."

Everyone turned to look at him.

"What Scotch didn't tell you earlier…"

"What!" The Inspector exploded.

Scotch raised a hand. "Inspector, give Otter the chance to finish, please."

The Inspector gave Otter and Scotch a scowl and then nodded. He sat down, but his frown didn't leave his face.

Otter shrugged and then continued. "The one thing your forensics experts missed, but which I got right off the bat, was the chemical traces that were left on the…uh…throats of the victims."

The Inspector sat up stiffly. "Chemicals?"

He eyed Flim. "Why didn't you notice this?"

"We did."

Flim gave Otter a suspicious look, which Otter returned with a sweet smile. "Unless you worked in the military like I did, you wouldn't be familiar with this one. Most police forces wouldn't by nature, either."

"What do you mean?" The Inspector demanded, curious despite his anger.

"In the last several years, the military has been using a chemical enhancement."

"What does it enhance?" The Inspector demanded, definitely interested now.

"Precision."

Otter sat down and nodded to Scotch.

"When Otter told me about the presence of the chemical, I did a bit of research in my spare time."

Otter commented, "Which means he didn't sleep."

Scotch shrugged. "Plenty of time to sleep when I'm dead now, isn't there?"

The men in the room broke into laughter—even the several women detectives who had kept a well-reserved presence to this point in time.

One, in particular, gave Scotch an appreciative look, lost on him. But not discouraged, she continued to examine him more closely now, as if seeing him for the first time.

"What motivated you to lose your sleep over the prior crimes, Mister McBride?" The Inspector asked.

"Pearl."

The room became relatively silent then. Everyone knew who Pearl was. They looked away from the forlorn look on Scotch's face. They also knew what her profession had been, and despite that, Scotch's feelings for her.

The female detective suddenly dabbed at an eye, as if feeling his pain. Scotch glanced at her, cocking his head questioningly a moment, then looked again at the Inspector.

"I would turn over heaven and hell to find her killer!"

Otter chuckled. "And the hell part he definitely got quite close to."

The men chuckled.

Scotch smiled faintly. He found it funny, but a bit off-key at the moment. He went on. "I asked Otter to check the results from Sir Flim O'Brian's autopsy reports, and then this morning after the head was also examined."

"And?" The Inspector inquired, getting a touch excited despite himself.

"Feldspar."

"Feldspar?"

"Yes. It is used principally as an industrial application for its alumina and alkali content. But in this case, a new process has allowed the military to use it to find a new military-grade purpose. To not only increase the efficacy of military-style weapons but their precision as well. Making them a deadly combination in today's modern age of warfare."

The female detective who had suddenly become interested in Scotch, spoke up, "Typically used by snipers the more frequently, because of their added efficacy and deadly outcome."

The room became filled with excitement as they considered the ramifications of what Scotch had revealed.

Both Scotch and Otter turned to look at her after the remark. She blushed but held eye contact with Scotch, which was not lost on Otter, who quickly looked away and pretended to be busy with his hands.

"Remarkable observation, Detective," Scotch told her.

She smiled, nodded, and then looked at her own hands, pretending to find something fascinating there all of a sudden.

Scotch smiled and then nodded to Flim. "No reflection on you that to you missed the connection, Flim."

Flim nodded. "None took."

He sat down, shoved his cape back over his left shoulder assuming his best Sherlock Holmes at rest pose, then took his pipe out to smoke, but didn't light it when the Inspector shook his head.

"So..." the Inspector finally ventured, thoughts boiling like hot water in his mind. "There is a third clue in this, I suppose?"

"Right you are, Inspector," Scotch admitted. He rose. "And now Otter and I are off to secure the last bit of information we need to tidy up this bit of a mess."

"What is that?"

"The name of the serial killer."

Scotch turned on his heels and exited the room, followed by Otter, who nodded to the Inspector and followed Scotch out.

"Otter, can you drive the car out front and meet me there?"

"Why?"

"I have a meeting with someone."

Otter gave his friend a puzzled look but departed for the parking to fetch the car.

Scotch turned around to face the conference room just as the female detective came hurrying out. She almost slammed into him.

He reached his hands up to catch her arms and give her support. "Sorry, I didn't mean to be in your way, Detective."

He let go, and she gave him a shy smile. "Detective Margaret Mallory."

He smiled. "I knew your father. A good man."

She got a sad look.

"I'm sorry; I didn't mean to distress you."

"No, no, no. It's not that. It's just that sometimes." She leaned so close he could smell the perfume behind her right ear.

He suppressed his shock when he realized he knew the fragrance. It was the one that Pearl always wore: sandalwood and roses.

He gave her a shocked look.

She dropped back a bit. "Are you alright, Detective McBride?"

"Please," he urged, recovering quickly, though feeling a tinge of sadness inside at the reminder of Pearl. "Call me, Scotch."

She smiled.

And then he remembered the young Detective who had made fun of him with the computer some years back. Fondly remembered.

Pearl flipped a waffle on Otter's plate. He immediately dribbled honey over it, then added a few strawberries and began eating.

Scotch watched his friend a moment with a smile, and then when Pearl tried to give him another, he shook his head. "Topped off, dear Pearl, my lady."

"Same." Detective Mallory told her when she glanced her way.

Pearl gave the detective a knowing smile, then nodded and headed back into the kitchen.

"She's a sweet woman," Detective Mallory commented, stirring her now cold coffee with her spoon.

She sipped it, made a face, and then got up. "I'll be back."

She headed for the kitchen.

Otter leaned towards Scotch and whispered. "That one's hot for you, Scotch!"

"Nah, not in your wildest dreams, sonny. She's just interested in my detective skills."

"Then why hasn't she asked me a single question all night?"

Scotch had no answer for that.

Otter smiled, took his plate, and headed for the kitchen. "I'm marrying Pearl!"

Scotch barked with laughter.

Detective Mallory came back with a steaming pot of coffee and set it down on a placemat. She sat down and then glanced at Scotch. "What was that about?"

"Otter fancies our new cook and roommate."

Detective Mallory grinned. "He'd be a fool not to. That one's one smart cookie. Speaking of which…"

Pearl came back into the room with a half plate of cookies and set them down. "Butterscotch and caramel oatmeal cookies."

"Where's the other half?" Scotch asked.

Pearl poked him with a finger on his shoulder. "You're the detective. You figure it out."

She laughed and then went back to the kitchen.

Scotch eyed the stack of cookies thoughtfully.

"I just might have made a mistake by letting Pearl move in with us."

"Why's that?"

Scotch cocked his head to look at Detective Mallory.

"They're both young enough to still want babies."

Detective Mallory barked with laughter.

Scotch and Detective Mallory sat on the front porch of 221 B Angel Flats, eyes on the stars overhead.

"You never did tell me where you were born, Detective McBride."

He looked at his palms a moment and then nodded. "Aye, suppose I haven't then."

She smiled. "You can be awfully evasive when you want to be."

He cocked his head to eye her quickly, and then look away. "I've been told that by many a woman."

"You're not a ladies' man."

"Question or statement?"

"Maybe both."

"Nar. Me the likes of women...we don't do so well together."

"You prefer men?" Detective Mallory asked in surprise.

"Not at all. I love men. As friends. No more." He sighed and then put his head into his hands.

Detective Mallory instantly realized she'd plunged into emotional territory with him. She tried to back off to give him room to breathe. "Unusual weather we've been having lately."

He still didn't answer.

She didn't look at him. She just said more. "I suppose it has something to do with climate change. All the scientists have been talking it up heavily lately."

Still no response.

"Whatever the reason, it's nice to have a touch warmer weather."

She finally looked at him.

His head was on his knees. He began to snore.

She smiled.

"Detective McBride, you're quite the romantic one."

She kissed him lightly on the top of his head, then gently pulled his coat up tighter about his neck and looked up at the stars again.

Her thoughts flew up to them with the wings of angels, and she could swear she saw a fluttering of stars that resembled wings for a moment before the vision fades away.

Scotch and Otter entered the small shop off Oway and Culbertson. Shadowy and dimly lit, it seemed more like a pub, even to the extent that a tall man with broad shoulders stood behind the counter. Wiping it down with a white cloth as if it were a matter of course and something he frequently did.

He looked up as the bell tinkled on the door.

"Chaps!"

Scotch hung back, and Otter went forward to the counter. He laid down a sheet of paper. "I need this. Fast!"

The man eyed the paper, squinting.

"Second, mate."

He reached under the counter.

Scotch and Otter both tensed at the motion, but the man came out with a pair of eyeglasses, which he shoved over his nose to read the paper.

He looked up at Otter.

"Not a common thing."

"I didn't expect it would be. How soon can you have it for me?"

"Depends."

"On what? Drew Pascal told me you had some."

The big man looked surprised a moment, then quickly pulled back together, turning away.

"As I said, it depends!"

The big man turned, composed again, and eyed Otter closely.

Otter stared back, totally untouched by the hard stare. "Have it your way then." He reached into his pocket and laid a hundred-pound note on the counter.

The man swept it off and into his right pocket. A slight smile touched his scarred lower lip, and for the first time, Otter felt a wave of fear. The man was on the edge of something he didn't want to deal with. That made a man quite dangerous.

He signaled Scotch with a hand behind his back.

Scotch patted his trench coat where his weapon was.

Otter nodded.

The big man was already on the way into the back and didn't see the gesture.

"Give me a minute!" He called as he ducked through a beaded curtain into the back of the shop and was heard moving boxes.

Scotch came to the counter. "What do you think?"

Otter shook his head. "We're shooting in the dark here, Scotch."

"As usual."

Otter shrugged and turned as the big man returned through the beads, leaving them banging together behind him from his shove through them.

He set down a huge box.

Must have weighed about twenty pounds.

"Twenty pounds of feldspar as you requested, matey."

Scotch came in close to the box and peered inside. "Doesn't look like the stuff we came for at all."

Otter shoved his face closer. "Sure enough, you're right."

Scotch suddenly began coughing quite hard. He struck the box by of feldspar, and it flew towards the big man.

He reached over to stop it, and Otter grabbed him by the arm. "Don't mind my pal. He's got terrible asthma."

"No problem, matey."

The big man reached under his counter and came out with a sealed bottle of water and handed it over.

"Thanks!" Scotch managed to squeeze out and then fell into another coughing fit.

He became wobbly.

The big man grabbed him to steady him across the counter.

Otter tapped the man on his back. "He's fine. Just let him have a moment."

"Whatever you say," the big man replied and let go.

Scotch gave him a grateful smile. "Thanks!" He wheezed.

He turned to leave. Otter followed him.

"What about your feldspar?"

"Keep it!" Otter replied and turned to leave.

The man watched them walking away, a puzzled look on his face. "What about your money?"

"Keep the change!" Otter said over his shoulder. "And the rocks."

They exited the shop, leaving a happy chime behind them from the bell on the door.

SURVEILLANCE

Detective Mallory shrugged deeper into her overcoat. The night had been warmer, but the morning air was brisk and biting. She had goosebumps up and down her spine and legs. Even on her arms and the back of her neck as well.

"Come on! Come on!" She urged the shut door. She was watching from across the alleyway on the fire escape. Hunkered down so as not to be too apparent in the shadowy section of the landing she was spying from.

The door finally opened.

The big man that Otter and Scotch had been checking out shut the door, locked it, and then scampered off to the right.

She smiled.

"Got you, blighter!"

Mallory dropped from the fire escape to the alleyway. Lost her balance a moment, until she felt a pair of strong hands steady her.

"Thanks!"

Scotch stepped alongside her. "It worked?"

She smiled.

Otter came to her other side. "Of course, it worked. The man was obviously a scam artist. Those stones were nothing more than granite with a bit of mica in them."

Otter pulled a small device from his pocket and eyed its face. A green arrow was moving away from what had to be their position.

"Shall we take a bit of a jog this morning?" Scotch asked.

Detective Mallory smiled. "Love to."

Scotch smiled back. "That was quite a lovely drop you did a few minutes ago."

"Been watching CSI and Jackie Chan movies since I was a kid. Learned a lot."

Otter put a hand up, and Detective Mallory and Scotch dropped back a step. He turned and motioned with a finger at the building on their right.

He made a hand motion indicating the fourth floor.

Scotch eyed the building.

"Fire escape?"

Detective Mallory smiled.

DANGER ON THE FOURTH FLOOR

Drew Pascal stood beside the window, the big man standing behind him. Nervous. Distraught. Worried.

His lower, scarred lip was quivering with fear.

"I'm going to have to stop selling to you, Drew. I don't like strangers coming to tell me you sent them, and they didn't."

Drew didn't turn around, kept to the shadows, his eyes on the street below. "I need you."

"I don't need the trouble."

"I pay you well. Very, very well."

"Money won't do me any good if I go to jail. The Yard is good. I don't want them yanking my chains when I got such weak links."

"What do you suggest I do then?"

"I've got another hundred pounds in the back of my shop. Come tonight. Midnight and it's all yours."

Drew turned around.

His face was like stone.

Cold and lifeless.

DANCING WITH THE DARKNESS

Scotch stood outside the door; hand on the doorknob as Otter stood to its left, prepared to stop anyone that might make a dash for freedom.

Scotch spoke, raising his voice as he did so. "Scotland Yard. Open up!"

Nothing.

Otter raised an eyebrow questioningly.

"Scotland Yard, Open Up!" Scotch roared even louder.

Still nothing.

Scotch nodded to Otter.

He kicked the door.

The door flew off its hinges.

Lying on the floor was the shop keeper, Drew Pascal. His head lay on the floor, eyes staring into infinity, his face frozen in horror.

Parts of him here.

Parts of him there.

Blood flooded across the floor from all the torn limbs and torso, pooling at the base of the window frame and slowly oozing towards the door.

The window to the room was open.

Scotch's eyebrows rose in alarm. "The fire escapes!"

Scotch ran back the way they had come, and Otter ran around the blood to the open window.

DEATHLY DESCENT

Detective Mallory hid outside the room, a level down, waiting for some indication she was needed. Wouldn't do for her to be seen. Might precipitate a rush for freedom.

She had her ears wide open for whatever sounds might be coming from above. She should have been listening below.

A thick hand grabbed her ankle and yanked.

She screamed!

WHO?

Otter looked out the window, the same time as Scotch looked up from the street level.

They both shook their heads.

DANGER

Scotch shook his head. No sight of either the Detective Mallory of the killer.

Otter shook his head too, but then he suddenly jerked back from view.

"God, no!" Scotch cried out.

DEAD MAN'S ROOM

Scotch rushed into the dead man's room and froze. Otter stood against the right wall, a blade tight under his jaw, the killer standing calmly next to him.

Scotch locked his eyes on the man endangering his friend. He put his right hand into his pocket and let it rest there.

"Mister McBride, I've been expecting you. Please make yourself comfortable."

"Thanks, but no thanks, laddie. I prefer the comfort of my feet. Attached, preferably."

The man looks at the dismembered Drew on the floor. "He betrayed me. They all betrayed me."

"All? Who's all?"

The man laughed. "I'm not giving you the grace of a confession."

"I'm no priest."

"And I'm not a sinner. They deserved to die. All of them."

Scotch's right hand clenched what he was searching for in his pocket.

"Don't draw a gun on me or your friend dies."

Scotch laughed. "I don't believe in guns."

The man frowned. "Pull your hand out slowly."

Scotch obliged.

Slowly.

As he withdrew his hand, it came out with a pair of balls attached to each other with a string.

"Toys?"

Scotch shrugged. "A man has to have something to do in his spare time."

The man laughed.

His blade cut deeper into Otter's throat. Beads of blood wet the edge of the blade.

"Don't do as he says, Scotch. He has no intention of letting either one of us go."

The man smiled warmly. "One never knows, does one? Unless they try." He scowled at Scotch. "Sit down!"

"Sure thing, matey!"

Scotch sat down. He began twirling the two balls about each other.

The man watched them with interest. "Very nicely done, Mister McBride, I congratulate you on your eye-hand coordination."

"Yes, this keeps me tip-top and ready to go as you yanks often say."

"You know I'm American?"

"Oh, come now, mate, you're wearing Nikes, and your British accent is atrocious. Even a child born here would know you're an imposter."

The man relaxed a bit. "You're every bit as smart as I was told you might be."

Scotch continued twirling his balls about each other. "I suppose. But I had been really, really smart, I wouldn't have let you catch me now, would I?"

"No, on that, you're right."

"Where's Detective Mallory?"

"Who?"

"The woman who screamed."

"I can't be in two places at once, Detective McBride. Never heard a thing, only your dumpy friend here mulling around inside, then leaning out the window."

He cut a bit deeper into Otter's throat. "Naughty, naughty. Never turn your back at an active crime scene."

Scotch grinned. "Otter's always been the impulsive one, haven't you?"

Scotch winked.

Otter groaned.

"I'm afraid he's unable to protest without me slicing his throat deeper."

Scotch shrugged. "Suppose so. Well, I guess you won't just lay down your knife gentleman like and surrender so we can end this?"

"Not likely. I have a plane to catch."

"What if you're late?"

"I won't be."

Scotch looked at the window, which the man had his back to. "Detective Mallory, I don't suppose you could convince him otherwise, could you?"

The man turned to look.

Scotch flung the two attached balls. They whirled through the air and wrapped about the man's neck. Startled, the man dropped his knife and made choking sounds.

He grabbed at his throat to loosen the strings of the balls, but they were too tight.

Otter chopped him on the side of his neck, and he collapsed to the floor.

"Good job, Otter."

Otter rubbed at his throat, looked at the pearls of blood on his fingers. "I love a good shave, but this one I could have done without."

The man on the floor stopped making choking sounds.

"Better untie the balls before he chokes to death."

Otter nodded and loosened the balls.

Scotch tossed a pair of plastic ties.

Otter threw the man over on his stomach, tied plastic cuffs to his wrists and ankles, and then got up.

"Where's Detective Mallory?" Otter asked.

Scotch frowned.

"That's what's got me worried."

"But you've caught the killer."

Scotch shook his head. "No, we've caught a killer. But he's not the Swish Killer. He hasn't a clue how to use a martial arts weapon, let alone a highly sophisticated weapon that hurls blades for bullets."

Otter's face paled.

Scotch nodded.

"She's been taken by the real killer. The man who severs his victims into parts."

"Then, she's as good as dead."

Scotch frowned deeply.

"Let's pray that I am not wrong in this, Otter, but I suspect not."

"Why?"

"Because it doesn't fit the MO of the killer. He likes to stalk his prey."

Scotch took the two attached balls and dropped them back into his trench coat pocket and sighed. "Now, we need to find out which plane the killer was taking."

The man on the floor opened his eyes and smiled. "You'll never know."

Scotch smiled. "Why is that, laddie?"

"Because he could never take his weapon on a commercial flight…"

The man-made a choking sound.

Scotch grinned.

He pretended as if he were tipping a hat to the man.

"And thanks for the clue!"

Scotch and Otter stood near the baggage area, watching as passengers entered the large handling area searching for their bags.

"Why here?"

"Just a suspicion."

An older woman, apparently eighty or so years of age, sat at a nearby bench, hunched over by the weight of arthritis and her waning years. She mumbled to herself like a person also losing their mind.

The Inspector saw her and frowned, but said nothing. He then nodded to several constables, who were all incognito, dressed in civilian clothes. They went to the east and west of the room.

Scotch saw the other two near the entrance and exits of the room.

"You're sure about this, Detective McBride?"

Scotch nodded to the Inspector. "Her life depends on me being right."

"Exactly."

Scotch eyed the man sternly. "I have never lost a man on my watch."

"Nor I."

Scotch looked away. "Yet."

Both men sighed inwardly at that. Yet. A big hole in their hopes. They both protected those they served as best they could. But both knew that death could reach out at any time and strike down a loved one.

"So why here?"

Scotch returned his attention to the Inspector, who was also not dressed formally. He wore a white starched shirt, a green tie, and a wool sweater, opened the top four buttons. His shoes were the only giveaway. Regulation and spit-shine polished.

Scotch shrugged. He didn't think this killer would pay that much attention. At least he hoped not. He wished he was right.

Casually, he glanced about. "I don't see anyone suspicious, do you, Inspector?"

"Not really. I don't even see where to start?"

Scotch smiled.

"Well, first, I would ask myself, if I were the killer, how I would know where Detective Mallory was going to be. Wouldn't you, Otter?"

Otter smiled. "More than likely."

"And second, I would ask myself how this killer would be aligned with the first one. Was the one who killed Drew Pascal the man we brought to justice earlier or was he merely a companion?"

The Inspector frowned. "Companion?"

"Aye, laddie. Companion. Let's look at this from the killer's viewpoint, shall we?"

The Inspector turned to look Scotch with a touch of doubt in the eyes. "Go ahead."

"What if the killer was not a random murderer, or even one with an agenda of vengeance…seeking to the right an old wrong, an old act of evil committed upon him or a loved one."

"That's quite an assumption," the Inspector said.

"Yes, but for argument's sake, Inspector, what if the killer was not a man of random acts, but of malignant purpose. Seeking to satisfy some kind of perverse pleasure or idea of perfection?"

"Somehow…perfection and perverse…don't sound like they could be friends in this case," the Inspector pointed out.

"True enough. And if we were talking about just any man off the street…"

"We don't know it's a man yet."

"…Or woman," Scotch amended himself.

"Yes?"

"What if this killer was a highly trained and skilled operative?"

The Inspector turned away to watch his men.

Scotch glanced at Otter, who winked.

Scotch looked at the Inspector again. "How would such a person have the information that brought the killer to the same shop that Otter and I discovered randomly through the yellow pages?"

"Forensics."

"Yes, forensics. But more."

The Inspector turned to Scotch. "Just what are you getting at...?" He frowned. "And what the hell are we waiting here for like a cluster of fools for a killer? We have no idea of whom he is or what he looks like."

"Well, actually we do," Scotch admitted with satisfaction.

"And what evidence do you have then?"

"First, forensics led us not only to the shop the killer used for his ultra-top-secret weapon but also to two men who needed such blades."

"And?"

"One hadn't a clue how to use the blades in the manner they were used. No prior history."

"But he killed the shopkeeper. He was there with the body."

"True enough, Inspector. But in a court of law, that is not evidenced enough. Not to put a man in the darkest of dungeons for the rest of his life."

"Then what is?"

"Who the man was working for. With."

The Inspector frowned, causing his forehead to wrinkle like waves on an oceanfront, and then pulled out his pocket watch to glance at the time. "I can't wait here any longer, Mister McBride, I have a planet to catch."

"I'm sure you do, Inspector."

Something in the tone Scotch used caused him to look into Scotch's face.

"Just what are you getting at, Detective? I can't be late for my flight."

Otter got a signal from one of the constables watching the carousel where luggage was being loaded onto a cart and then taken to the waiting jet airliners.

Otter left the two men.

The Inspector didn't notice. His eyes were fixed on Scotch, who was holding his attention now that he had pulled out his two string-attached balls and was beginning to play with them, twirling them about.

"Will you stop playing with that toy?"

"Oh, it's not a toy at all. Australia's aborigines use it frequently to capture game and ward off evil men's intentions."

"Well, there's neither one here, Detective."

"Oh, but I think there is."

The Inspector sighed deeply. "Very well, then. I'll bite. You say you have some idea of who the killer is…?"

"I do indeed."

"Go on then."

"The man is someone no one would ever suspect of such dark and diabolical deeds."

"Yes, yes."

"Someone who is a citizen of outstanding character, known and respected in his community."

"And?"

"Perhaps even a public servant."

The Inspector looked away from Scotch. But Scotch could see he was tensing upon sight of Otter and several constables coming towards them, carrying a piece of luggage.

"What's the meaning of this?" He demanded. "That's my luggage!"

Otter threw down the piece of luggage and its lid popped open, spilling blades across the slick, highly polished floor.

Passenger let out cries of alarm as the sharp things skidded among them.

Then what was at the bottom of the black luggage container came into view.

The Inspector gasped.

"What the devil?"

"Indeed, what the devil?"

Scotch nodded to the constables on the right and left walls, and they came running. The two who had carried the luggage rushed forward.

The Inspector made a dash for freedom, knocking over Otter as he scampered hurriedly towards the exit from the luggage room.

He got about ten yards and ran past the older woman with arthritis, who suddenly put her foot out. He tripped on it as she awkwardly rose and faltered a few steps, and then a loud whistling sound came from behind him.

He found his ankles both suddenly locked together by two balls, and he was flung violently from his feet to the polished floor. He flew about five yards, slamming into luggage and passengers, who screamed in alarm.

He whipped around to grab at the balls, tying his ankles together but had only just reached for them when several strong hands gripped his arms and lifted him to his feet.

Scotch and Otter walked up.

"Thank you, Constables."

The two constables nodded and stepped back, two more quickly applying plastic cuffs to the Inspector's hands and then his ankles.

Camera phones and cameras began flashing the event unfolding in the room.

Heathrow would never be the same.

"You won't get away with this nonsense," the Inspector told Scotch. "I've been framed."

Scotch smiled. "Hey, you! You old woman! Get your bonnie bottom over here!"

Several older women turned about to look, startled by Scotch's tone.

An old woman, who had been bowled over by the weight of her years, suddenly stood up, threw off a gray wig and white shawl, then tore at the theatrical mask that hid her real face.

Detective Mallory grinned at Scotch. "Now that's no proper way to treat an old granny now, is it, Detective?"

He gave her a warm, welcoming grin. "I trust your abduction went according to plan?"

"Had it not, our dear Inspector here would be off to bonnie America."

The Inspector was dragged away.

"Wait!" He ordered.

The constables looked back at Scotch, who nodded.

"I want to know what gave me away."

Scotch smiled. "Now that would be telling now, wouldn't it?"

The Inspector gave Scotch a look that could kill if such a thing were possible. Then he nodded to the men holding the Inspector. They hurried him towards the exit. There, several more constable waited next to a police wagon. The constables the Inspector to the wagon and pressed him inside, a bit more roughly than they might have otherwise. Shut the door, then the constable driving the vehicle drove him off, blue light flaring and siren wailing.

Scotch sighed and retrieved his bolo from the floor where the constables had dropped it. He frowned. "The string is a bit on the worn side. I'll have to replace it."

Otter took it from him. "I know just the man." He walked off.

Scotch turned to Detective Mallory. "Well, that's that, I suppose."

"That was fun."

Scotch frowned. "I hardly call arresting the Inspector who runs Scotland Yard fun."

"I do. That blaggart was always putting filthy hands on me."

"And that was the clue I did not dispose to him," Scotch admitted, as he turned to leave.

She followed next to him.

"You saw him?"

"Yes, when he thought I wasn't looking. I have a keen eye and am not incapable of seeing from the back of my head upon occasion."

She laughed and put an arm through his, surprising him.

"Well, all that may be true, but I have to say this, you really know how to show a lady a good time."

He frowned. "What lady?"

She smacked him lightly on his arm. "Scotch!"

He grinned.

221B ANGEL FLATS

The dinner that night was the best ever. Pearl and Otter fired up the old oven. Came out smiling with the finest roast Scotch had ever seen. Lamb with sliced apples and pears smeared over it and sprigs of clover and cinnamon to add flavor and bite.

He pushed back from the table, setting his fork across his plate and eyeing the dessert he had made—Scottish pudding. A blend of milk boiled rapidly, with fresh chocolate chunks, raisins, and still more cinnamon added to the mix and some flour to give it body.

"I'm not sure I can defeat this enemy," Scotch admitted as Detective Mallory spooned a healthy serving into a silver bowl for him and handed it over.

But he took it anyway. He just didn't touch it right away. A knock came at the front door.

"I'll be right back."

He ducked from the room. Heard speaking with someone, and then he returned and pulled a harmonica from the inside of his jacket. "Anyone mind?"

Pearl sat down, after taking away all the empty plates with Otter's help, and Otter sat next to her, which she smiled about as usually he sat next to Scotch.

Detective Mallory nodded. "Love to hear you play."

Otter groaned. "Famous last words, my dear."

Scotch grinned. "Surely, my best friend doesn't think so little of me music, does he?"

"He does!" Otter admitted with a grin.

Pearl chuckled. "You two never stop, do you?"

"Only when we are off striking for the pearly gates on the heels of Saint Patrick and his lambs," Scotch told her with a bit of a wink.

She laughed.

Scotch began playing.

An hour flew by—first, Beautiful Dreamer and then Love in your Eyes. Eventually, ending with the rowdy piece, Rosette the Pub Girl. Music flowed like magic from him. Each song filled with whimsy and bouncy, energetic moves. Finally, after dragging out the dancing tune as long as he could, he settled in for a long series of blues in Cee.

Otter glanced at Pearl, who was fascinated by the music. "Isn't that American?"

"It is. Scotch learned it from a fellow there when he visited about a year or so ago."

Detective Mallory had her chin on the palms of her hands, listening with her eyes closed. "Harmonica Blues Samuel."

Scotch suddenly stopped.

His eyes popped open, and he looked at her. "You know, Samuel?"

"Grew upon him. Daddy used to play him all the time on his fiddle."

"You play the fiddle?" He asked.

"Don't get me started," she begged.

Otter ran out of the room for a moment and came back with a fiddle.

Detective Mallory eyed it like an animal fierce enough to tear her throat out and carefully put it to her shoulder, the bow ready to play.

She glanced at Scotch. "Once I touch the bow, the demon of the blues takes over."

He touched her arm gently. "I'd like to see that."

She gave him a new look, one that he had seen once before and was both genuine and piercing to his heart. He looked away, thinking of his lost Pearl for a moment. Still, when Detective Mallory broke into her first song, "The Blues Gone Wild," fiddling up a storm in G Flat, he was consumed. She put an overpowering zest into each stroke of the music. He found himself, without thinking, playing his harmonica lustily along with her.

BAKER STREET STROLL

Scotch wore a scarf and a Scottish cap that hooded his mop of hair nicely in shades of gold and yellow. Detective Mallory strolled next to him along the sidewalk.

He pointed at his place from across the street where they stood.

"It's said that the great Sherlock Holmes once lived here."

She smiled. "You love that man, don't you?"

"Aye, muchly, but he's a hard legend to live up to."

She turned fully to him. "Is that what you want most in this life? To live up to his legend?"

He looked at her; briefly, his head cocked slightly to the right, then away. "I'm not so sure anymore what I want to do with the rest of my life."

"Let's keep walking," she requested.

"Anything for a fine fiddler, even if a bit off-key on that last piece."

She nudged him playfully. "I was following you; you rogue."

He grinned. "Like I said..."

They broke into laughter.

As they walked the sidewalk, a light breeze came up. Mallory shrugged her shawl closer about her shoulders but didn't complain.

"So, tell me, when did you finally suspect the Inspector?"

"I didn't."

"Didn't what?"

"He's a clever man. Threw me off me game righteously."

"Most killers are. I feel sad for all the men that looked up to him, though. It must be crushing for them to see their hero go down like that."

"Scotland Yards are the finest, dear Detective. And this is just one day more of many such days in their lives. Those who love the law and live by it are constantly faced with the drama and trauma of changes. Not all of them sweet. And many, quite bitter."

"Sometimes, you sound more like a Merlin the Magician than a detective."

Scotch chuckled. "Another hero of mine."

"You do tricks?"

"Oh, not like that. I do real magic."

She laughed.

"No, seriously."

She laughed again.

He smiled.

"So not at first then, we'll skip the magic if you don't mind."

"Not at all, me lass."

"Then...?"

"When Otter and I discovered how the blades were delivered. We also were led to the manufacturer of the ignition used for the blades."

"And?"

"Made in only one place."

"Where?"

"The Inspector's home town. Gloucester."

"Why would that make you think it was him then? Many people live there or have been born there."

"Aye, very true."

He stopped and turned to her, the hint of a grin, touched with genuine sadness. "But one thing those others didn't have in common with the Inspector."

"What?"

"His blood."

"Oh?"

"You see, forensics came back with a sample of blood that was not the victims. It was not identifiable at first."

"How did you finally identify it then?"

"The law demands that anyone who purchases a certain combustible material have on record files of their birth, and…"

"Their blood," Detective Mallory guessed.

"Yes, DNA. "

"And then?"

"And then it was just a matter of setting him up as we did, though it was a close call for you and a lost cause for poor Drew."

He looked sad again.

"But he wasn't clean in this."

"No, but no one deserves to die like that. No one!"

"So, you checked the DNA sample against the national base and…"

"Inspector Dublin."

She nodded.

"Well, sad as that is, at least we've removed a mad man from the streets of London."

"I truly hope so," Scotch said mysteriously.

"Why are you talking like that? We both watched him led to a jail cell?"

Scotch gave her a solemn look. "Now, I don't want you to be frightened."

She shivered at the look on his face.

"Now, I am frightened."

He looked away; his head cocked at that weird angle it always was. "The front door I answered earlier."

"Yes?"

He looked at her again. "He's escaped."

A shadow fell across both of them—a huge one.

Scotch spun around.

Otter and Pearl were strolling towards them so close together that the shadow thrown by them from the streetlight enlarged it and made it seem gigantic.

Scotch let out a sigh of relief.

"Well," he said.

Otter grinned. "Want to join us?"

"Why not?" He asked grinning. "We've not a care in the world, do we Me lass?" He asked Detective Mallory.

She hesitated a moment when he offered his arm and then took it with a smile.

"None whatsoever!"

www.ingramcontent.com/pod-product-compliance
Lightning Source LLC
Chambersburg PA
CBHW061536120726
48001CB00004B/1581